Screaming Into The Ether

(and other tales)

by

Laura Lavajin

BACK ROADS CARNIVAL BOOKS
mattspencerauthor.wordpress.com

ISBN (print): 9798218334529
ISBN (ebook): 9798218334536

"Kids Say The Weirdest Things" first appeared in *X4* © 2016

Printed in the USA

For Pixie and Marlowe

Acknowledgements

A shoutout of thanks to some folks without whom this volume would not have been possible: Garret Cook, Aubergine Evans, Estelle Janisieski, April Kelley, Jessica Kenney, Cheryl Ploof, and John Short

CONTENTS

FORWARD

by
Matt Spencer

Any claims to objectivity on this editor's part would be a transparent falsehood, so I won't waste your time or mine bullshitting you, dear reader. Instead, I'll start by saying that I wish this volume wasn't so slim, that there was more surviving, completed fiction by Laura Marie Janisieski (1979-2023) (Laura Lavajin, as she wished to go by on the page, should her writings ever see professional publication), that she'd written more…Hell, more than anything, I just wish she was still here with us, that she'd won a few more of the painful inner battles with which she struggled all her life, which took their monstrous toll over the course of her final year…of that last part, out of all love and respect, the less said here the better.

Either way, here I am, left with more questions than answers, a lot of strong, unresolved conflicting emotions, so many haunting regrets and what-ifs…and the best way I have left to honor her, which is to see her writing published.

For eight years, Laura was my great love, my world, including an all too brief marriage, after which

1

our friendship somehow survived, before we yet again became on-again/off-again lovers, right up (almost) to the end.

During those turbulent times, she sometimes tapped into a knack for speculative fiction writing…Hell, she'd already dabbled in it and always showed a natural flare for it, whenever some spark set something ablaze that burned through the cold cobwebs of her crippling depression and anxiety. During those bursts, she became an artistic force of nature for a while.

In fact, one of her earlier efforts was how we first met. She'd written a surreal, dreamlike piece of dark fantasy/horror, and asked a mutual friend of ours if said friend knew any professional authors of similar genre persuasions who might take a look and give her any pointers.

Her friend was like, "Well, just so happens…"

As of this writing, that story sadly seems not to have survived, lost to time several computer crashes ago, despite all my best efforts to unearth it. It was upon reading it, though, at that first enticing glimpse into her inner world and taboo-shattering imagination, that I already started falling for her.

Let me put it this way: a while after our relationship began, we watched the movie *Wayne's World* together. At the point where Wayne says of his love-interest-to-be, that babe Cassandra, "She will be mine…Oh yes, she *will* be mine!" Laura astutely turned to me with a sly smile and said, "Why do I get the feeling that that's what you were thinking when we first met?"

Guilty as charged, ladies and gentlemen of the jury!

A few years later, she began picking at the title novella of this volume, and that's when she really began to hit her stride. With her heart of bottomless empathy and compassion, one of Laura's most deeply held characteristics was her passion for environmentalism and animal rights advocacy. Not that she was one to let all her sweetness and idealism dampen her twisted sense of humor or taste for the macabre (one of the reasons we worked as a couple, when we did).

She was like, "How about an old-fashioned alien-invasion story, except where the aliens are an industrialized, corporate intergalactic society who treat us humans the way we already treat other species, not to mention the whole planet?"

Yes, Laura was one of *those* outspoken vegans, but I assure you, dear reader, lay aside any misgivings that you're about to read some tiresome, preachy, humorless screed. Laura pulled out all the stops in spinning a ripping, gleefully depraved yarn of Bizarro sci-fi horror lit, full of vividly realized imagery and characters (both human and extraterrestrial) that often leap off the page. She left no stone unturned while painting her harrowing, apocalyptic hellscape, by turns morbidly comedic and graphically, gut-wrenchingly, sometimes outright heartbreakingly nightmarish, occasionally in the same breath.

In the process, it might just make you stop and rethink a thing or two from a new perspective, about this world we all share, as often only the best, most daring speculative fiction can, in ways people bitching at each other over social media could never dream of. That's my girl!

The result is not in any way restrained or subtle, but then, it's at heart the kind of tale that would no more benefit from restraint, subtlety, or any other contrived artfulness than would an old Chuck Jones Merrie Melodies cartoon…except where if someone gets an anvil dropped on their head, their brains are likelier to splatter all over the place and they stay dead…or in the case of Laura's World, get incinerated by a distressed alien's combustible fart.

But you needn't take my word alone for it.

After Laura bounced the novella off me, I recognized its publishable potential, and hence saw it into the hands of my own editor, acclaimed Bizarro/horror author Garrett Cook. After his editorial expertise helped Laura punch it up for maximum effect, he for a while advocated for its publication through Eraserhead Press. Sadly, nothing came of that.

Laura also bounced the story off my longtime friend and mentor, the late great "Lonesome

Cowboy" Bill Hilburn.

Bill gave it a read and told me over the phone, "Shit, man, I felt like I was reading something straight out of Harlan Ellison's *Dangerous Visions* anthology!"

To which I responded, "Yeah, that's what I said!"

As to the rest of the stories presented here…Like I said, I wish there were more of them, but what we have speaks for itself, so we're left in frustration at just what else could have been.

How Laura ever came to write the tale *Blame It On The Drugs*, I can't exactly recall, aside from the escalating opioid crisis that we witnessed unfolding every day around us, both within our community and throughout the country at large in the news (which, as of this writing, has only continued to get worse, with no relief in sight). What stuck out then about the tale, and still does, was the unsettling sense of authenticity she captured, of the inner workings of a world with which she (at the time) had no such up-close-and-personal firsthand familiarity.

Once again, my lady's innate, unsettling prophetic instincts asserted themselves, it seems.

Funny thing about BIOTD…It came the closest of any of Laura's works to actually seeing professional publication within her lifetime. Not only that, it was accepted into the same issue of the same prestigious neo-pulp magazine as a collaboration between the aforementioned Bill and me…right before said magazine, *Econo Clash*, folded after the pandemic hit. Go figure.

So unless you were there during the one or two times Laura got up the guts to read the story aloud at an open-mic performance, you're experiencing it here for the first time.

The delightful *Excerpts From Cinch's Diary* was born of a writing prompt from the aforementioned Garrett Cook, something to the effect of "Think of some colorful character from your community, speculate, exaggerate, and do something wild and over-the-top and crazy with it."

Subsequently—from our musings over a local lovable n'er-do-well barfly who'd somehow gotten into a hammer-wielding altercation with some bully, while for unexplained reasons wearing a dress—Laura produced her own cockeyed little take on the superhero/costumed-vigilante subgenre.

The final tale here, *Green Wives Say The Weirdest Things*, holds an extra special, no doubt extra biased place in my heart. It was Laura's own sequel to my story *Kids Say The Weirdest Things*. I embellished the latter from an anecdote she told me, about a weird interaction she once had with the neighbor's kid out in her garden while I was at work at my day-job.

Since I, as the husband, wrote the first story from the wife's point of view, Laura turned it about and told what happened next from the husband's point of view. I've shamelessly included KSTWT in this volume, not for Laura's tale failing to stand on its own, but because, well, in a way, it's the closest we ever got to a successful writing collaboration.

On that note, I figure it's time I got out of the way and let Laura's storytelling do the talking.

It's your time to shine, my love.

Screaming Into The Ether

Prologue

The Quaestui hunter twisted its long, hairy, plated snout into a semblance of a grin and sniffed the air. It rotated the saucer-shaped protrusions at the ends of its long, thin antennae, sending out thousands of tiny sonic squeaks to take in as much of the scene as possible in under a second. The prey had fallen here. The ferns were broken and many lay flat. Blood clung to the leaves that stubbornly reached for the sky despite their broken stems. The hunter flexed his huge, plated nostrils and breathed deeply, savoring the smell.

The trail led off to the left. The hunter dropped to all six limbs and followed at a leisurely trot. Every so often, there would be another sign that its prey was struggling. A bloody print marked where he had leaned against a tree, probably to catch his breath. Further on, he had fallen again. The hunter paused and picked up a blood-covered leaf. It lifted it to its mouth, and a long, thin, elastic tongue crept past two rows of sharp teeth to flick across the leaf. Invigorated by the taste of blood, it scanned around for the trail, and finding it, walked on four limbs in the direction it led.

~

The man fell again, this time onto the side the creature had stabbed him in with one of its long, exoskeleton-plated fingers. He screamed as hot iron seared into his ribs. He had to make it out of the woods, find somewhere to hide. He groaned and picked himself back up. Blood drenched his side from the torso down. He put his hand futilely over where he'd been stabbed and tried to start running again. The wound oozed blood between his fingers. He took a few stumbling steps, then collapsed again. This time he couldn't get up.

His breaths grew quick and shallow as he heard the creature approaching through the woods. He reached for the gun that was no longer on his hip. He had expended all his bullets at the beginning of the chase. He'd shot at it where the eyes should have been, and the creature had toyed with him, falling to the ground and struggling for a moment before it lay still. The man had approached the body, thinking he had killed it, even though he had seen no bullet holes in its thick exoskeleton. The creature had waited until he was close, then it swung one of its six long limbs, knocking him to the side. He had rolled and jumped back to his feet, dodging another limb in the process. He'd used up the rest of his bullets, dodging and running between the trees, then finally thrown his gun at the creature. When the creature had caught up and stabbed him, he'd thought it was over, but instead the creature had pushed him, as if it wanted him to run. So he had.

As the creature came into view, the man tried one last time to get up. He collapsed onto his back in defeat as the alien rose up to its full twelve-foot height over him. It just stood there a moment, flexing those cups on the ends of its antennae. Then, slowly, the creature placed a six-fingered hand onto the man's chest. He struggled to squirm away. The alien raised another arm, then shot it down towards the man's face, quickly and deftly scooping out an eyeball with two fingers. The man screamed as the creature ate his eyes greedily, one by one. Finally, the creature picked him up and bit off the rest of his head, crunching the skull and sucking out the brains. The alien sat, happily munching on the man, eating its fill. When it was finished, the alien tossed the remainder of the body aside and made its way back to its shuttle.

~

The Quaestui hunter flicked switches on the dashboard of its shuttle craft. As it lifted off the ground it switched to autopilot on a course straight back up to the main ship. Today had been a good hunt. The feral stultus on this planet weren't the most challenging, and their weapons were amusingly harmless, but it felt good to just get out, chase down, and have lunch in the woods. There was nothing like fresh meat, straight from the body.

Part One

Captain Terb emerged from his stasis capsule, stretched all six limbs two by two, yawned, and farted. The echolocation sensors in the ends of the pair of long, thin, plated stalks protruding from his hairy exoskeleton told him his co-captain, Sebon, had yet to awaken. Good, he'd have time to have a cup of capulus before he had to deal with any telepathic intrusions into his six-lobed brain. He pressed a button on the wall next to the capulus maker and waited for the stimulant beverage to brew. Five long minutes later, he groggily carried a hot, steaming cup in his fourth six-fingered hand onto the bridge and sent tiny, sonic squeaks at the display panels. The ship's sensors indicated they were within the solar system of Farm Planet A3427H. They had arrived ahead of schedule; the rest of the massive fleet were still a week behind them. *We must have hit a glitch in the wormhole along the way. Good, maybe I can slip out and get in a little hunting before we have to get to work.*

Terb felt a telepathic mind probe. *Good morning, Sebon.*

Morning Captain! How was your vacation? You went to a hunting planet, right?

Yes, Hunting Planet Delta 367D. The daughter wasn't

too thrilled. She thinks it's inhumane to hunt species who've developed advanced societies, even if they can't communicate properly. Funny, she doesn't have a problem eating them from the supermarket!

Ha! thought Sebon, *kids these days, I tell you. They'll think they alone can discover a way to communicate with a species that can't mind-probe. Ridiculous. How'd it go?*

Thern and the kids ended up having a great time on a tour of the planet's tectonic structure. You know her and geology. The rock collection grew so much, I had to pay for an extra shuttle to get it all back home.

How was the hunting?

Positively thrilling! On this planet the dominant stultus had some primitive technology. My guide explained that they'd just developed the ability to leave their atmosphere and visit their moon when a Quaestui probe discovered them. They lived in expansive above-ground structures, had even developed transportation, and the best part — weapons!

Oh my goodness!

Yes! On the third day, I stalked a large male of the species for a while. It had some kind of rudimentary projectile weapon that it fired at me multiple times, but of course the little pellets barely tickled! The damned thing only had four limbs, so I decided to give it a sporting chance with a head start. It led me into the remnants of one of their cities. It was a grand chase. You'd be surprised how fast they can run with so few limbs! I finally cornered it on the fourth floor of what appeared to be some sort of manufacturing plant, in a restroom. The creature fought to the end! The scream when I ripped its head off almost burst my antennae!

Wow! Sounds like an adventure, Captain!

It sure was! Where did you go this year?

Another beach planet.

Uninhabited?

Yeah, just sun, sand, food, drinks and beautiful women!

Terb checked the ship's sensors again, saw that everything was on course, then led Sebon back to the captain's lounge. *You and your women. Find any good dates?*

Sebon poured herself a cup of capulus and sat at the table. *I met the most wonderful girl at the bar. Her sonic probes of my body caught my attention right away when I sat down. I sent her a suggestive mind probe, she started squeaking with giggles. We hit it off after that. Went back to my room after a day at the beach, and well, she had the most supple fingers on each of her limbs, if you know what I mean…She almost knocked my exoskeleton off!*

I'll bet, say, did you have any plans for breakfast?

I was just thinking I'd have the computer thaw some…

Hold that thought! How about some fresh skullberries? The stultus on Delta 367D have twelve of them!

Twelve! What luck! Such a delicacy, skullberries! I would love some, thank you!

Terb pressed another button on the wall, and a panel slid back revealing a kitchen setup. He pulled open a door and removed a capsule which let out a blast of nitrogen when he opened it. He took a frying pan from another cabinet and began heating it on the stove. *How do you prefer yours?*

Over easy, thank you. Sebon sipped her capulus thoughtfully. *I heard the stultus on this planet only have two skullberries each. We'll be catching a pretty penny on them from this planet, that's for sure.*

The dominant stultus on this planet already farm other pecus species, but for some reason they don't use the skullberries! How bizarre! I read the report before we departed. I ordered several shipments of skullberry extractors, so our workers won't have to scoop them out with their hands. They should be delivered when the rest of the fleet gets here. Terb tested the pan with one heavily armored finger. Satisfied, he tipped the capsule, and twelve golf-ball-sized eyeballs plopped onto the hot metal. Instantly they began to sizzle. Terb opened a drawer and aimed his antennae into the clutter therein until he echolocated a spatula. *We're ahead of the rest of the fleet, care to join me for a bit of hunting when we arrive?*

No thanks, Cap. Hunting's your sport. I might take a shuttle and scope out where we're going to be building our slaughterhouses. Whereabouts are we landing, anyway?

The east side of a large continent in the northern hemisphere. Our ship was assigned to a mountainous river valley area where the dominant stultus farm a larger pecus species for dairy products. We're to be landing on a town where the inhabitants seemed more docile than in other areas, according to the scouts.

Sounds like we'll have it easy for a week then. I know stultus weapons are laughable but they do make an awful lot of vibration. Hopefully they don't attack the ship with them. Ahhhh those skullberries smell wonderful. Do you have any salt?

Of course! Terb flipped six eyeballs, over easy, onto a plate and handed them to Sebon. *Enjoy!*

~

Byort woke from stasis as stiff as if he'd stood on two legs for the entire voyage. His massive jaw gaped in a huge yawn before he ran his flat, elastic tongue over his two rows of sharp, sleep-gunk-coated teeth. *Damn, did I forget to brush my teeth again? Shit, better not breathe on anyone.* He crawled on all sixes out of his stasis tube, stood up, and bee-lined for the workers' restroom.

Behind him, rickety worker stasis tubes slid open with squeals and thumps. The air filled with the vibrations of farts, yawns, and groans. Quaestui workers emerged, many of them as tired as the day they'd gone into stasis. Byort felt a familiar telepathic signature as he returned from the restroom. He sent an enthusiastic mind probe. *Wolta! You old fart! How've you been?*

Wolta turned and thought *Byort! You bastard! How was the mining planet job?*

Long story, want to catch up over some breakfast?

Wolta clapped Byort on the back with a clack, and they headed for the cafeteria. Once they were in line, grabbed a couple of trays of offal, and echolocated an empty table, Byort thought to Wolta *Don't let anyone else mind probe into this conversation, okay?*

Yeah man I hear you. So what the hell happened?

Byort chewed a piece of pecus liver. *It was bad. There was an explosion. A lot of workers died. It was faulty equipment. I know it was. They made us sign non-disclosure agreements.* He swallowed and belched as he continued. *I didn't even bother feeling all the bumps on the contract. I knew it was bullshit and it basically said if we told anyone about it they could sue the hair off our exoskeletons. I watched my buddy die under a pile of rubble. A boulder the size of a house had fallen on him and cracked right through his thorax. He begged me to tell his wife he loves her as he died. Fuck, the crap bonus they gave us survivors barely covered his funeral. I paid, of course. His wife was stuck with eleven kids from their last egg sac. She was scared. They might have to move to a low-income planet. She's got family but they're in one of the colonies in an entire other galaxy. You know how expensive it is to travel intergalactically for anything other than work these days?*

I know. That's bad, man. Didn't the miners have a union?

Nah the union went bust right before I got the job with FodiaCorp. They made it out to be a great thing that I didn't have to pay dues for some asshole to whine about the thickness of the toilet paper in the bathrooms.

Haha, Wolta laughed mentally. *Yeah, my last job was in terraforming and construction on a low-income housing planet. Man, that place was a wasteland. The only thing that could grow there was moss, lichen, and fungi. They said the air still contained enough methane to give us cancer, but the bosses didn't care. Those bastards got gas masks any time they had to leave the ships! I wouldn't be surprised if they start moving destitute Quaestui in before it's even at safe levels. When our contract was up, they were bringing in the pecus for the residents to farm and eat. Some species with eight skinny legs, no brains, but a lot of meat!* Wolta picked up a small organ that resembled a kidney. *Unlike whatever species they're feeding us on this ship, huh?*

~

The Quaestui worker transport ship came in low over a small stultus town, and settled slowly, crushing several blocks of quaint brick buildings. Stultus gathered around the ship in a multitude of wheeled vehicles that screamed strange ululating vibrations. Attempts were made to dig under the ship, presumably to find the stultus bodies that inevitably had been crushed. The Quaestui didn't worry too much about wasting stultus at the initial landings like that, there were always plenty more to farm. Stultus weapons soon lined up next to the ship, but the Quaestui didn't worry about that, either. Their ships were usually invulnerable to any and all stultus weapons they had ever encountered in their eons of exploring the universe for planets to exploit. The few planets they had ever scouted that had species with superior weapons, well, they were smart enough to leave those planets be.

The stultus seemed to make crude attempts at vibrational communication, both via bodily vibrations emanating from their mouths and by tapping on the ship's doors, but they had been determined long ago by the scouts to have no telepathic abilities. Quaestui had no interest in communicating with their food, anyway. Any species that couldn't mind probe was, well, quite frankly inferior.

~

About a week later, inside the ship, on the bridge, Captain Terb paced irritably on four limbs. He hadn't had a chance to get out and go hunting. Workers were complaining about boredom and lack of variety in the cafeteria. Sebon wouldn't shut up about the damned beach and women. Every little vibration was driving Terb up a wall.

Captain?

What now? Terb snapped back with annoyance.

Sebon flinched. *The rest of the fleet have arrived into orbit around the planet. I guess it's time to get to work. Shall I mind probe the local carrier captain?*

Finally! Terb wasn't about to miss the fun. Hundreds of stultus had gathered around the ship, and what seemed to be one of their queens had arrived earlier this week. Killing a queen on a new planet could reap a fat bonus. The stultus had set up some sort of platform outside the ship's huge bay doors. *Stupid stultus.* Terb wondered how such a species had even managed to build crude shelters, much less multi-story buildings, vehicles, and weapons. *How can they even see anything without echolocation? Those crude grunt-like vibrations they produce don't even echo properly.* Terb laughed to himself, picturing stultus milling around with building materials, bumping into everything and each other until they found the spot they needed to place the next piece.

Sebon interrupted the Captain's musings. *Captain?*

Yes yes. Find out who's in charge up there and invite them aboard after to feast on a queen!

Captain!?

That's right, there's one right outside our ship.

Why would they send their queen right to us? What a dumb species! They should be as easy to farm as their pecus!

Terb felt a fellow captain's mind probe and responded affirmatively.

This is Captain Ligus of Carrier ship Theta 6097. I see you arrived early. Status report?

Terb stretched his mouth into a huge, toothy grin. *Ligus, you old son of a pecus! How have you been?*

Terb! How are things down there you old coot?

Fantastic. The stultus have brought their queen right to

us, can you believe it? This is going to be an easy planet.

Queen? Well I'll be! I imagine you've already called dibs.

Of course, but you're welcome to share with me after. I'll even save you a skullberry!

Haha sounds like a plan! We're set to touch down shortly at your location. It'll be good to see you again! I can't wait to catch up!

Me either. I'll eagerly await your arrival.

~

Quaestui carrier ships contained small fighter ships, transport ships, and first-wave workers, unlike Terb's ship, which carried the long-term workers. Workers were also technically fighters. Quaestui didn't need any special training to invade a planet. Their thick exoskeletons could withstand a blast that would take down a hillside. The average Quaestui stood about twelve feet tall. Their massive jaws could bite the head clear off just about any species of stultus that had a head. Pure carnivores, they ate their meat raw, with the exception of skullberries, which were considered a delicacy cooked. They were very prolific and efficient farmers, and had established thousands of farming planets in this galaxy alone.

Farming planets consisted of three types — beverage farms, meat and dairy farms, and feed farms. Beverage farm planets grew capulus beans, and various grains which were fermented for alcohol.

Feed planets were terraformed to grow a grain called trital. Trital was then shipped to meat and dairy planets to fatten up stultus and pecus. Really, all stultus were ultimately pecus, but Quaestui distinguished the two by how docilely the species would go to their deaths. Pecus were generally more docile but stultus sometimes had to be tamed and/or partially eradicated before they could be farmed. Still, stultus tasted better when they put up more of a fight, or at least the Quaestui thought so.

Most meat and dairy planets were temporary contracts, because the population created by farming stultus and pecus so intensively would cause the planet's atmosphere and biosphere to collapse within a few decades at the most. Many stultus species that farmed their own pecus had already polluted their planets so badly that by the time the Quaestui probes discovered them, there were only a few short years of life left in them. Such was the case with Farm Planet A3427H. The atmosphere there was so far gone that AgriCorp had estimated only ten or twenty years before total collapse. Despite how slowly they grew, it had still been determined profitable to farm the planet's stultus, however, instead of just killing them off immediately and farming faster-growing pecus.

~

The mind probe went out planet wide. Begin the

initial invasion.

Terb quivered with anticipation as the giant ship doors slowly whispered open. He elbowed Sebon. *Are you ready for my favorite part?*

As ready as I'll ever be, Captain. She watched through the widening crack as the fighter ships flew out of the carrier's bay doors and lined up over the stultus weapons.

As the doors slid to a halt, the stultus queen came walking across the platform, both upper limbs outstretched, toward the captain and co-captain stepping out of the opening. Several stultus with weapons chased after it. A telepathic chuckle resounded through the workers lined up behind them.

Are they sacrificing their queen? thought Sebon to Terb.

Terb grinned, began walking, and opened his four upper arms to embrace the queen back. A concussive blast as the fighter ships took out the stultus weapons blew the queen into his grasp and tossed the others aside like paper. Widening his grin, Terb bit the head off the queen, grimaced, and spat. The head landed with a wet thunk at his feet.

Ugh! That tasted like it was marinated in exoskeleton wax and my wife's perfume! Terb exclaimed to whoever had an open mind at the moment. He spat again and noticed Sebon happily chewing on an arm. *They don't all taste that bad?*

Quite delicious, Captain!

Why would they douse their queen in… They tried to fool us! Terb echolocated a fattened stultus off to the side with a strange contraption aimed at his head. For some reason this one wasn't fleeing right away. He ran to the creature and disarmed it with a flick of his finger. Before the stultus could take one step in any direction, Terb flipped it on its side and took a bite out of the torso. *Mmmmm that's better.* He picked fabric out of his teeth, and looked around for his next victim.

Some Quaestui workers were busy erecting corrals and the rest were chasing down fleeing stultus, eating some and throwing others into giant sacks. If a stultus struggled too much, sometimes biting off a limb would immobilize them, or kill them. No big deal, there was just another body for the good meal they always had after the initial invasion. A headless body landed at Terb's feet as he turned to chase down another stultus. He felt a wet plop on the back of his head.

Gotcha, Captain! Sebon grinned, revealing a skullberry balanced between her teeth.

Terb laughed, picked up the stultus head, and sucked out the remaining skullberry. Translucent fluid spurted from his lips as he chewed and grinned.

A stultus with a weapon ran across the platform, a loud, deep vibration bellowing from its throat as it fired at Terb. The bullets made a tinking vibration as they glanced off him and hit the ground. The stultus stopped, dropped its weapon, and turned to run. Terb skittered over on all sixes and bit off a lower limb as they both crashed off the platform. He spit out the leg, tossed the body aside and ran after the next nearest creature.

~

Three hours later, the telepathic all clear resounded through the small town. Quaestui emerged from piles of rubble, carrying straggling stultus by the limbs, hair, clothing, or sometimes by the string of guts hanging out of their torn abdomens. Workers closed the corral gates on hundreds of live stultus, while others gathered the dead and stripped and gutted them in preparation for the arrival dinner.

Terb stood with Ligus and Sebon on the remains of the platform the stultus had originally erected to present their false sacrifice.

The only thing that makes the taste of that queen worth it is the fat bonus I'll be getting on my next paycheck, thought Terb.

Sebon laughed. *Who'd have thought they would try to fool us like that. Maybe they thought we would get one taste and just turn around and leave?*

Stultus don't think, scoffed Terb. *If they could think we would be able to communicate with them.*

True, but don't they seem able to communicate amongst

themselves somehow?

That's just the hive mind, for lack of a better word. Did you see how they scattered once the queen was dead? Chaos. Without a queen, they're no better than pecus. Tastier, though.

Ligus chimed in. *Indeed. I hear this species only produces one offspring at a time. You'll need to breed all the females if you're going to farm this planet efficiently. Save a few robust males for ejaculate, and set up an intensive artificial insemination program. Scouts observed the stultus dealing with the pecus this way, so they should adjust easily enough to having it done to themselves.*

Terb grimaced. *You concentrate on doing your job, Ligus, we'll worry about the farming. You get to go home and wait for the scouts and probes to find more planets to farm or mine.*

Don't act like you'd love sitting around doing all the red tape after an invasion, Terb. Then there's the planning, calculating numbers of fighters, ordering construction materials and equipment, and so on…

…And you get to go home from the office and boink your wife every night. I'm stuck here managing the farm for the next ten years!

Hahaha touche, Captain, Sebon piped up.

Ligus poked Sebon on the arm. *You stay out of this, co-captain. What do you say, my sergeant has informed me that dinner is prepared. Shall we?*

The captains and co-captain descended the platform towards the carrier ship.

Mmm I hope they saved us extra skullberries. I could go

for a pair, poached, thought Ligus as they boarded the ramp to his ship. *How do you like yours, Sebon?* He extended an arm for the co-captain.

Why, over easy, of course… Sebon entwined an arm with Ligus' as they entered the captain's lounge.

So, what's next on the agenda for you two? Ligus' mind probe was relaxed as he pulled out a chair for Sebon with one arm, a chair for Terb with another, gestured at Terb to sit down with a third, and unwrapped his fourth from Sebon's arm, all at the same time.

Terb replied as he sat, *As you know, this continent will be dedicated to stultus farming. We're to round up all the pecus in the region and ship them off to the continent to the south of here. We'll begin converting all existing farms to house stultus and build new facilities in prime locations. This region is ripe with milk farming. It will take very few alterations to convert existing pecus milking machines to fit stultus females. We're also to have several slaughterhouses in our region. Sebon here has been formulating a breeding program to maximize profit and cut down on waste.*

Sebon perked up at the thought of her name. *Yes! Stultus on this planet produce an average of one offspring every twelve of our home months. It comes out to about ¾ of a local year here. If we breed the stultus females approximately once a year, milk production will keep up with the rate of their pecus using half the space to raise them! The breeding stock will replenish at approximately the same rate as the primary dairy pecus on this planet, as well. We'll maximize profit on stultus and pecus meat and dairy for at least the next ten*

Quaestui years, assuming the planet's atmosphere holds out.

There's a smidgen of feral creatures on this planet, as well. I suggested allowing trophy hunting, but the Grand Minister of AgriCorp insisted it's not profitable enough to bother with. All the more for me! thought Terb excitedly.

Ligus agreed. *We have three months of construction and minor terraforming to attend to before we leave this planet to you, perhaps I can join you for an outing?*

I would love it! Ahh, here's dinner!

Three Quaestui workers came in bearing platters piled high with choice cuts of stultus. A fourth carried a bowl heaped with skullberries, still sizzling from the frying pan. The workers placed the dishes on the table, bowed, and left.

Sebon spooned several skullberries onto her platter of meat. She squeezed the thick, viscous, translucent liquid from one onto a rack of ribs, tore off a section and held it in the air.

Terb and Ligus each picked up a leg from their platters.

Cheers!

To Farming Planet A3427H!

The room filled with the vibrations of tearing flesh, smacking lips, loud gulping, and blissful belches.

~

Byort pulled a flailing stultus from the main corral

and tore off its clothing with one ripping gesture.

Male!

He lightly flung the creature into the left of the second set of corrals they had erected the day before.

He roughly grabbed another stultus and tore off its raiments.

Female! This one he tossed into the corral to the right.

Wolta stood beside Byort, doing the exact same thing.

Male!

Male!

Female!

Male!

Fem-hey this one looks like it's already been bred!

Nah, that one's just fattened up nicely. Maybe I'll just take a bite…

Don't even think about it, if you get caught eating a breeder, they'll take it right out of your check!

Oh fine. Wolta tossed the female in with the others.

I worked a farm planet when I was about two hundred thirty years old, where the stultus had six different sexes, Byort reminisced. *It was a boneless species, and their genitals were hidden in a pouch that was hidden between one pair out of fourteen tentacles. Sorting was a nightmare…*

A mind probe went out to all workers at once. *LUNCH!*

Awright! Byort dropped the stultus he had just

grabbed back into the corral and bee-lined for the ship.

Wolta threw the male she had just stripped into the left corral so hard its leg snapped and it let out a screaming vibration. She caught up to Byort moments later.

I sure hope they still have leftovers from the arrival! It'll be back to offal before we know it!

I don't mind offal, thought Byort. *Joke's on the Captains, it's more nutritious, too!*

Yeah well, we deserve better nutrition working these hours. The least they could do is give us an occasional brain or skullberry.

Ha! Brains and skullberries are damn expensive, they wouldn't waste them on the likes of us!

When I worked on Feed Planet W98G3L back in my eighties, they gave us each a brain and a poached skullberry once a year on our work anniversary. That was back in the days of the agricultural union. Remember such a thing as vacation time? I went to a camping planet once with my eighth husband. My twelfth brought me to a beach planet. It was heavenly. What I would give to have another week in the sun. Wolta sighed mentally.

Your twelfth husband, was that the one I met at the spaceport that time?

Nah, that was seventeen, Sidl. Twelve, I mean Thox, was managing a store on a brothel planet at that time.

I can't keep track of all your husbands, Wolta, no matter how many times you tell me their names and numbers.

You're lucky, you only have to keep track of one wife!

I don't know how you women do it, thought Byort affectionately.

How many of Thild's other husbands have you met?

Just three of them. Our work schedules line up sometimes, so we'll have a cup of capulus here and there. Sometimes something a little stronger, if Thild approves.

Haha why wouldn't she?

She's been on this health kick lately. Only organic, trital-raised pecus meat, no advanced society stultus. She's worried about the planets where the stultus pollute themselves. She goes back and forth on drinking. One day a glass of organic plasma wine is good for you, the next all booze is evil. She's been like this ever since she worked with that flakey new-age lady on a vacation planet. They cleaned rooms together, so every day she was filling Thild's mind with "clean eating this" "positive energy that".

Sounds like a load of hooey. My husbands can eat and drink what they want, as long as they don't wake up working on a brothel planet!

Haha! Byort plucked the last remaining gallbladder off of his tray and tossed it in the air, deftly catching it in his mouth. *It's just about time to get back to work.* He mentally groaned.

Wolta leaned back and stretched, then cracked the knuckles on four out of six hands. *Yeah, I suppose. I wonder what we'll be assigned to once we're done sorting stultus?*

I hope I get into a slaughterhouse. Not much more

satisfying than slitting a throat, and feeling all that blood spray out into barrels for plasma wine. It's like I'm doing a good deed, helping lift Quaestui spirits, you know what I mean?

Haha that's charitable of you!

As Byort and Wolta made their way back toward the corrals teeming with stultus, they felt a stern mind probe.

If you two could be more gentle with the stultus, that would be great, thought Vayo, the shift supervisor. He sipped his steaming cup of capulus as he continued. *We really need to cut down on waste, and an injured stultus is useless for breeding. You injured a prime piece of breeding stock, and now we have to slaughter it because of a broken leg. So yeah, just remember to lightly toss, liiiiightly tooooossss... By the way, you two will be working in a slaughterhouse next week.* Vayo jerked his antennae suddenly. *Oh, a mind probe from the new regional manager, excuse me. Back to work now! Tut tut!*

Wolta thought mockingly as she and Byort resumed walking, *Be gentle with the stultus! It's not like there's billions of them on this planet to eat!*

Byort let out a mental snort. *It's not like Vayo doesn't get paid to walk around feeling superior and drinking capulus.*

Slaughterhouse, that will be fun. It's good to work on a farm planet in general.

You bet. It makes me feel good to know I'm providing food for Quaestui throughout the galaxy.

Wolta snorted. *You just like to sneak scraps, you greedy*

cretin!

You caught me! They arrived back at the corrals. Byort grabbed a stultus by the head and ripped off its clothes. *Female!* He tossed it gently into the rightward corral.

Male! To the left.

Female! To the right.

This one is ambiguous. Do you have an internal organ scanner?

Here you go.

Thanks. This one's sterile. Toss it in with the males to be sorted for slaughter.

Female!

Female!

Male…

~

Within three Quaestui months of the first wave arriving, stultus planet-wide had been just about defeated, rounded up, sorted, and, depending on age, either immediately slaughtered, put in feedlots to fatten, or sent to dairy farms and breeding facilities. Mountains were leveled, vast concentrated farming operations and slaughterhouses were built — for mainly stultus on three continents, mainly pecus on the remaining three habitable continents of this planet. Coastal waters that weren't too polluted were transformed into vast sea-pecus farms. Quaestui fishing ships dropped huge nets all over the oceans to round up remaining feral sea-pecus for processing. Unfortunately the stultus on this planet had already fished their oceans almost to extinction. The Quaestui wouldn't let what was left go to waste, though, of course.

Quaestui were very efficient at slaughter. They ran their modified slaughterhouses like an assembly line, in pretty much the same way the stultus on this planet had run them when they slaughtered pecus. They were even able to repurpose existing primitive structures.

Quaestui wasted no parts of the stultus or pecus, either. Tendons, ligaments, hooves, nails or claws, and cartilage were boiled to make gelatin, which was very popular mixed with grain alcohol, or to fill giant tubs with to wrestle in on brothel or casino planets. Skullberry aspic was a popular dessert on vacation planets as well. Skins made great fabric, and were tanned and used to make carrying sacs, weapon cases, mattresses, and any number of other useful household items. Bones or exoskeletons, depending on whether the species had one, were ground after the marrow was extracted into a fine powder that was then made into dishes or mixed into concrete. Bone marrow itself was packaged and sold as a breakfast pate. Hair and feathers provided an extract that was the main ingredient in exoskeleton wax. Bile was very popular for perfume. Blood was divided into plasma from which a cheap but tasty wine was brewed, and platelets which were coagulated and stuffed into intestines for blood sausages. Fat was used to fry skullberries, and was also another ingredient in exoskeleton wax. It was also boiled down for mechanical lubrications.

Manure didn't even go to waste. It was shipped to feed and beverage farm planets for fertilizer. Trees were clearcut while terraforming, and were made into paper and furniture. The Quaestui a made thick paper, which was used mainly for embossed business contracts and newspapers, which were much more temporary than the plastic sheets used for history and literature.

Nor did Quaestui abandon a meat and dairy farming planet when the atmosphere collapsed. There was still oil and minerals to extract, oceans to pump and desalinate, stone to quarry! Many a mining company would begin bidding for rights before a planet was even farmed to extinction. After a decade or two, once there was nothing left of the planet to exploit, finally the Quaestui would label it Mortuus, and leave it and its winds to howl into the vastness of space.

~

Byort and Wolta arrived at the slaughterhouse for their shift on a fine fall day. They made their way up the ramps to the fourth floor. Byort clacked Wolta on the back as she veered left to her post on the disassembly line. He then continued to the receiving area, where he had been assigned to stun the stultus as they were herded down the ramp from the roof. He stretched his top two arms, then picked up his captive bolt gun. He mind-probed the shift supervisor that he was in place. Shortly, screaming vibrations echoed down the ramp from the roof as stultus were herded down with long, electric pecus-prods.

Byort grabbed the first stultus by the shoulder and quickly shot it in the head with the captive bolt gun. The stultus went limp and Byort tossed it to the next worker, who picked it up and hooked its foot onto the conveyor rack, and sent it down the line. Byort didn't even notice. He had to work fast. He didn't always stun the stultus properly before tossing it to the next worker, and it would emanate screaming vibrations until the third worker slit its throat.

Wolta was down the line at the gutting station. The worker before her slit the abdomens open, and she reached in and cut out the internal organs and intestines, so they hung out for the next workers to extract. Sometimes a stultus was still alive at this point. Wolta would giggle at the thrashing and the gurgling vibrations they made. A stultus came down the line with one of its skullberries hanging out by a thread. She plucked it and ate it quickly. She sent

Byort a mind probe saying thank you and cut the intestines. Before she swallowed, she had gutted seven more stultus, the line moved so fast.

After Wolta's post, the next worker in the line finished slicing the skin so that it could be peeled off easily by the next two workers. Once the carcasses were skinned, the subsequent work stations would begin cutting off limbs, slicing the torsos in half, and so on. Finally, the line descended to the bottom floor, where cuts of meat, bones, offal, marrow, and all the other bits were sent down the conveyor belts to be sorted neatly into shipping containers, and sent to various packaging and processing plants.

~

Captain Terb paused, sending thousands of tiny sonic squeaks per second from the saucer-shaped depressions on the ends of his antennae, scanning the echoes for the slightest change in his surroundings. Suddenly he felt a barely perceptible vibration of breathing to his left. His antennae focused in that direction. *There, behind that tree.* He dropped to all sixes and crept slowly toward the feral stultus he and Captain Ligus had been tracking for three hours. Ligus circled to the right.

Suddenly a crashing vibration alerted Terb to flatten to the ground. A huge log, through which spikes had been driven to impale whatever might be in its path, swung down and grazed his back. *Haha that tickled!* he exclaimed mentally to Ligus. He reached up as the log swung back, and deftly caught it with one hand. He gave it a yank and the ropes that it had swung from, as well as the branches that those ropes had been tied to, came crashing to the ground.

Ligus let out a laugh vibration that whistled through his teeth. *Clever, aren't the little bastards?*

They do come up with some interesting tricks, I must admit. It does allow for a more exciting chase, indeed. Which way did our game head, by the way?

I think it…

The stultus dropped from a branch onto Ligus' back. It wrapped its legs around his neck and reached behind it. A pair of bolt cutters slid from a pack on its back. Ligus stabbed at the stultus with two hands and grasped it by the torso with two more. The stultus clamped the bolt cutters onto Ligus' antenna and squeezed. Ligus screamed mentally as he lost his grasp on the feral creature's head and torso. He swung an arm at the stultus and drove a sharp finger into its back, just as the stultus drove a huge knife into the hole left by the antenna and into Ligus' brain.

Ligus collapsed onto his abdomen as the stultus fell off to the side. Huffing from the pain of the wound in its back, it ran deeper into the woods.

Terb howled! His back hunched and his echolocator dishes folded to slits. He dropped back to all sixes and stomped in the direction the stultus had taken. He easily followed the scent of blood before he came to a chain-link fence that had partially collapsed into the field that lay beyond. The stultus was running jerkily towards a building next to a large hangar. Terb stepped over the fence and ran on four legs at a gentle gait. He didn't want to hurry this creature's death. He wanted it to pay for what it had done to Ligus. He wanted to hear and feel and taste and smell its suffering. He slowed down when he was twenty feet behind the feral stultus. He followed it into the building on all sixes, stopped to sniff the air, then went up the stairs to the right. He followed the smell of blood and the vibration of heavy breathing, through a door into what had once been an office of some sort. The feral stultus sat against the wall behind a desk. It aimed a small projectile weapon at Terb's antennae and fired. The shot glanced off Terb's forehead and ricocheted into the wall. The stultus collapsed into a spreading pool of its own blood.

Terb walked over to the stultus, picked up a leg with two hands, and snapped the bone. The stultus' scream vibrated soothingly against Terb's antennae. He broke the leg in another place, then ripped off the leg at the knee. Disappointingly, the stultus appeared to faint. Terb picked up the body and flung it against the wall. Blood splashed back onto him as he reached for the body again and swung it again and again into the wall. A splatting, sucking vibration resounded as the corpse shit itself, which then stuck to the wall, which then stuck to the corpse, which then stuck to the wall again as Terb flung the stultus body into it again and again. The wall began to smash and crumble.

Finally, Terb dropped the body and sat on the floor. He held back a mental sob. All of his memories of Ligus flashed through his mind as he placed his head in four of his hands. After a moment, shaking, he slowly stood and took a deep breath. *I have to get his body back to the shuttle.* He took a few more breaths, and resolutely walked back down out of the building, and through the field to the fence. As he climbed over, he felt the vibration of a stick cracking in the woods nearby. He instantly whipped his antennae in that direction and echolocated another stultus, fleeing in the direction of Ligus' body. Terb dropped to all sixes and took off after it. He gained quickly on the stultus, and as Ligus' body came into sight, he was almost within ten feet of it.

Suddenly, something dropped from the trees and surrounded Terb, tripping him and causing him to tumble head over hands for several feet, tangling him in a flurry of arms and ropes. *A net! The stultus caught me in a bloody net!* Struggling, he only served to entangle himself further. He tried to rip through the net, but it was woven of strong, lightweight, flexible metal cables that he could not break. *I can't let these animals get the best of me!* Terb breathed deeply and tried to calm himself. *Think.* Terb slowed his movements and began methodically pulling at the net, trying to find the edge. A cable was pulled tighter, binding his arms closely to his body. *How the hell could this happen? I have to get out of this. I will kill these useless creatures and savor their skullberries!*

Two stultus dropped from the nearest trees. A third stultus, no, several more stultus emerged from the trees around Terb. Some of them grunted and whispered to each other. Three of them slowly approached him from the rear. Terb grew still. He began to panic and tremble. *What are they going to do to me?* The stultus in the lead pulled out a small, thin object and placed it in its mouth. More incoherent vibrations echoed from its mouth as it raised another small object to the first and pressed a button, producing a tiny flame. Just then, Terb let out a gigantic stress fart. The gas instantly caught flame and incinerated the stultus. The two others that had been behind the first ran around in circles, flames engulfing them, screaming vibrations emanating from their throats, their arms flailing. Other stultus ran to them and tried to put them out. Terb realized the fart had blown a hole in the net. He pushed his lower left arm through and grabbed a stultus by the head, squeezing until its skullberries squirted out between his fingers. Another stultus chopped futilely at Terb's arm with a sharp weapon. Terb squeezed until he was sure the stultus was dead, dropped it to the ground, and reached for the stultus that had attacked his arm. It jumped out of the way and four more stultus threw metal cables around him and tightened them until Terb could no longer struggle at all. He made panicked clicking noises as he thought to himself, *How could this have happened?*

The stultus waited until a vehicle with a long, flat platform on the back arrived. Terb frantically sent futile mind probes at the stultus. *Please, you don't have to do this, we can work something out, please!* The stultus showed no indication that they even noticed. Terb was loaded onto the back of the vehicle and tied down. Ligus's body was strapped down next to him, and the stultus vehicle set into motion.

An hour later, Terb felt the vehicle slow to a stop. He slowly stretched his antennae as much as he could in his bindings, and discovered he was inside a large building. Several stultus roughly unstrapped Terb and pushed him off the back of the vehicle. He landed with a thud that knocked the wind out of him. He felt a screaming stultus kick his exoskeleton several times until the others pulled it away. He struggled futilely against his bonds several times, but the net and metal ropes held tightly. The stultus milled around Terb, sometimes seeming to argue amongst themselves.

After a while, a few of the more angry stultus stormed off, and the remaining stultus pulled out a strange tool, which they plugged into a socket in the wall. Terb felt a high-pitched vibration as the tool came on. Two stultus held onto his arm as they untied it, and the stultus holding the tool moved toward him. A shrieking vibration rang out as the device came into contact with the exoskeleton surrounding the soft flesh of his armpit. Pain seared into Terb's consciousness and he lost his breath in what would have been a scream if he'd had vocal chords. The tool cut through the joint and his arm fell to the ground. Blood gushed from the wound. The stultus cut through the net around his next arm, and the others grabbed it and stretched it out for the tool. Terb's breath screamed out of him and he clenched his teeth so hard he bit through his tongue. Blood filled his mouth and he began to choke and cough. The white-hot pain seared through his body like lightning. He felt like he would split in half at any moment. The blood drained.

This must be what the stultus feel like in their last moments, he thought as his consciousness faded to nothing.

Part Two

Janine held her cigarette in her mouth as Thomas dismembered the bug with the bone saw. Neon-yellow blood gushed from the two gaping holes where its arms had just been, and pooled at the ground in front of her feet. The second arm fell to the ground. She took one last drag of her cigarette and tossed the butt into the puddle. "You done? I think it's dead."

"That would be the point," snapped Henry. "The things can't talk, so why keep 'em alive?"

"Lucy doesn't seem to think that's the case, she thinks we could communicate with them somehow if we tried."

"Lucy is delusional. The things are giant bugs. They must communicate through chemicals, like ants. How the hell are we supposed to talk through chemicals? I'll tell you how, give me a vat of acid to toss these bastards into, that's all I want to say to them." Henry's demeanor went from sarcastic asshole to sugary sweet within a second. "You got a cigarette?"

Janine stepped back as more blood sprayed towards her, when Thomas cut into the third arm. "Yeah. They definitely communicate amongst themselves, somehow. Probably through those antennae." She handed Henry a cigarette.

Thomas finished sawing off the third arm. "Are you going to help me get this net off?"

Janine lifted the net on her side of the bug and helped Thomas slide it off. "I don't know where the hell we would keep this fucker if we kept it alive anyway!"

"No kidding." Thomas walked around to the other side of the bug. "This is a warehouse garage, not a jail." He started cutting into the fourth armpit.

Janine picked up a pair of bolt cutters from the workbench and walked to the alien's head. "Thank fuck Johnny finally found a way to kill them quickly." She placed the bolt cutters around an antenna and squeezed. A slight well of blood leaked out around the blades. The antenna fell to the floor. Janine picked up a screwdriver and drove it into the hole.

"Hey, relax, it's already dead." Thomas cut off the fifth arm.

"I know, just letting out some frustration. Fucking Johnny is dead. So are Arturo, Neil, and Sally. Bobby and Jenny are badly burned. Gibson doesn't know if they're going to make it."

Henry walked over and plucked the screwdriver from the antenna hole. "Poor fucking Johnny. I can't believe he got killed by an alien fart!"

"It's not something to joke about, Henry." Thomas finished cutting off the final arm, and walked around to the bug's rear. "The thing seemed to know what it was doing. We need to make sure these things don't have weaponized gas sacs." He began cutting a line up the creature's abdomen.

"C'mon Tommy, I gotta make light of things or I'm gonna go crazy."

"It's disrespectful, Henry." Janine cut off the other antenna and picked it up.

"Hand me that crowbar?" Thomas put out a hand towards Henry.

"Yeah, here. I'm not disrespectin' nobody Janine. I just got my own way of handling things."

"Well just, keep it between us, the others might not understand."

"Okay, boss." Henry walked over to a mini fridge and pulled out a beer. "Thank gahd we ain't drank all this shit yet. Can't wait to get a brewery up and running again once these buggers get the hell out of here."

"They're not going anywhere. They're fucking farming us."

"Speaking of which, Henry, would you go see how Kalinda is doing with the bomb making?" Thomas pried open the bug's abdomen and inspected the intestines. "I don't see any gas sacs. I think this thing really just had to pass gas at the worst possible moment." He began cutting out the internal organs. "Three hearts, four lungs, one stomach, one liver…I don't know what this is…Let's take a look at this famed six-lobed brain." He began cutting open the skull.

Janine waved the antenna she was holding at Thomas. "Have you heard from Keene?"

"Not in the past week. Last I knew, they were planning to take down a dairy farm. Liam over there said they'd been scouting it for weeks, and had a solid plan to get in there and get out all the girls, then burn the place to the ground."

"I hope they did, I hope they did."

"Well it's been nothing but radio silence from them since I last talked to Liam. Honestly, I'm getting worried."

"I'm sure we'll hear a great big cheer on that radio when we bomb the shit out of the Brattleboro slaughterhouses." Janine tossed the antenna to the side and untied her apron.

"I'm sure."

~

Janine fell into her bunk with a satisfying thud and sighed. It had been a hell of a day. They had captured a live bug! She still couldn't believe it. She couldn't believe Arturo, Sally, Neil, and Johnny were gone, either. Bobby and Jenny were probably lost, too. "Six people, six more people gone," she muttered as she reached for a photograph tucked into the bottom of the bunk above. It showed a smiling Janine, with her brother and niece. Her niece had been six at the time, and they had all just gotten back from trick-or-treating. That had been six months before the bugs arrived. Her name had been Kara. She was a butterfly for Halloween. The next day, Kara had asked Janine to hang the wings on her bedroom wall. They were still hanging there when the bugs' ship landed on downtown and crushed their apartment building. Maybe Kara had taken them down and was dancing around with them strapped to her back right when the walls came crashing down around her. Maybe she had been dancing with her daddy. Janine liked to think that their last moments were happy, that they went quickly, that they weren't trapped helpless under the rubble for days, slowly dying of thirst.

The day the ship arrived and crushed half of downtown Brattleboro was a sunny Saturday at the end of April. Janine was working at the Price Chopper supermarket on Canal Street. Around two pm, everyone in the store heard what sounded like heavy thunder. They didn't think too much of it. A thunderstorm in April was unusual, but not unheard of. Until a driver from the pizza place they shared a plaza with ran in, screaming about the gigantic space ship that had just flown over. Janine had laughed, until her manager ran out of his office pulling up his pants, screamed about an alien invasion, ran out the door, got in his car, and promptly crashed it into the front of the building when he put it into reverse instead of drive.

Janine had run into the office and looked at the TV. Fox News was showing footage of a huge spaceship slowly moving north over the University of Massachusetts, Amherst. The newscast cut suddenly to live from downtown Brattleboro.

"Shep, the ship touched down right on top of Brattleboro, Vermont just after two pm today. Emergency crews are on the scene to search the rubble for survivors. It doesn't look to me like they'll be able to get under that ship, Shep. I'm being told four blocks of downtown Brattleboro were crushed under this huge spacecraft that arrived here on Earth today."

"Is there any sign that anyone, or anything, is going to come out of the ship, Nancy?"

"I've seen no sign of movement from the ship since it touched down minutes ago. Hold on… Yes, yes. I'm being told that we're going live to the Rose Garden for a statement from the President."

"My fellow Americans, today is a monumentous occasion. The aliens have seen how great we've made our country. Of course they came to the United States first, we're the best! The best! I tell you, they wouldn't have come here first if Crooked Hillary had been elected, that's for sure!

"Tragic. It's a tragedy what happened to all those people. My thoughts and prayers, thoughts and prayers.

"Against the advice of my trusted advisers, I plan to greet the aliens when they emerge from their ship. Air Force One leaves for Brattleboro shortly. Did I mention this day is monumentous? Monumentous occasion. Monumentous."

"The President speaking from the White House Rose Garden. Our fearless leader plans to embrace the aliens with open arms. What do you suppose they look like, Kelly?"

"Well, they're white, obviously…"

Janine switched off the TV and ran out of the office, stripping off her work apron and flinging it aside. The spaceship had landed right on top of downtown! She lived downtown with her brother and her niece… Oh my gahd it was Saturday, they would be home…

Janine ran the entire way down Canal Street to downtown. Just before Malfunction Junction, the police had set up a barricade. She tried to run through it.

"Miss, you can't go in there."

"But my family…"

"Miss, we're doing everything we can to find survivors." The police officer gently pushed Janine back behind the barricade.

"Tim! Kara! No!" She fell to the ground, sobbing. Then she remembered the ship. Slowly, she looked up, tears streaming down her face. The entire northern sky was blocked out by gleaming, silvery metal. About fifteen stories tall, the ship had come down on top of Main Street, crushing four blocks northward from the Co-op parking lot. It had sunk partially into the ground, obliterating the hill and anything that might have been beneath. It looked like it might end somewhere up by the Post Office or Grove Street. Huge double doors took up most of the side that faced the Co-op. There didn't appear to be any windows. The entire ship was as smooth and reflective as the surface of quiet water.

"Please, we live on Elliot Street."

"Not no more, you don't. Move along."

~

Almost a week had gone by, and the ship hadn't uttered so much as a squeak. Janine had been crashing at a coworker's on South Main Street, by the cemetery. The regional manager had insisted on keeping the store open, and told her she would be fired if she didn't come in. She told him to suck it.

Every day, she had walked through the cemetery, taking a flower here, a flower there from arrangements left by grieving relatives. Then she'd go down to the barricade and place the flowers under the photo she had taped to the barricade of her, her brother, and her niece. It had been in her wallet and was all she had left of her family. Then she would go to watch with hundreds of others, expectantly, hoping to catch a glimpse of whatever sort of creatures had apparently crash-landed here on Earth. The President had arrived later that first Saturday, and was holed up during the day in a bulletproof Hummer limo parked ostentatiously in the middle of Malfunction Junction. The military had long since taken over for the locals, and had brought in tanks and missile-launcher vehicles. A tent city in the Co-op parking lot teemed with official activity. The town had erected a platform outside the huge doors of the craft, lined with U.S. and Vermont flags. Each morning the press jostled with the early risers for the best spots behind the barricade.

Now it was the next Saturday, and Janine arrived bright and early downtown. She unslung her backpack and pulled out a thermos of coffee. By now she was sharing with the police officer who had initially snubbed her. "Good morning, Bobby."

"Morning, Janine. How's Matilda?"

"Oh, you know, she's still going to work, like the boss insists."

"That's crazy. I mean, I understand me having to work, I'm a cop, but Price Chopper? Come on…"

Just then a sound like thunder filled the air. Janine and Bobby the Cop looked up at the sky as another spaceship arrived over the town. This one appeared about the same size as the first.

"Oh shit! This one's gonna crash too!" Bobby jumped behind the barricade and ducked.

Janine was transfixed. She couldn't move other than to grip the barricade with both hands, as if holding on for dear life would save her life.

The second ship slowed at the last second, then gradually lowered, crushing another four-block radius of Brattleboro. Bobby stood up slowly.

Gigantic bay doors began to open on both the new ship and the first one. Smaller ships flew out of the newly arrived ship and arranged themselves in a line hovering over the Co-op parking lot. Janine immediately noticed the President running to the stairs onto the platform. Secret Service members ran behind him as he scaled the stairs and slowed down to a brisk walk, spreading his arms to embrace the aliens emerging from the ship.

They were hideous. Janine's first impression was that they were giant twelve-foot-tall insects, but with gnarly snouts with a lot of jagged teeth. Instead of eyes, they had two large, armor-plated antennae, with what looked like satellite dishes at the ends. Their black exoskeletons were coated in a scattering of coarse black, brown, or pale-yellow hairs. Each of their six legs had six long, jointed fingers. They wore no uniforms, not even a shred of clothing at all.

The first alien out of the ship and onto the platform carried no weapon. It extended its four upper arms, as if to embrace the President back. The last thing Janine saw was the creature opening its mouth, and two drool-covered rows of sharp teeth glistening in the morning sun.

Suddenly, there was a gigantic blast as the smaller ships fired on and took out all the perimeter of weapons and military that had gathered in the Co-op parking lot. The concussion blew Janine off her feet, and her hands gripping the barricade caused her to fly off her feet, get blown out straight, then fall flat on her face on top of Bobby. Glass shards and concrete chunks narrowly missed her. The fall knocked the breath out of her. As she lay recovering, a fine layer of dust settled all over her body. The photograph of her and her brother and niece drifted slowly down, and landed right in front of her face. She instinctively clutched it. Coughing, she stood. The bugs were swarming out of the ships. Some had weapons and were grabbing people alive and shoving them into giant sacks, some didn't and were merely killing anyone they could get their hands on.

Janine and Bobby were good, fast runners. It probably helped save their lives. The other thing that saved their lives was that the aliens were in no real hurry. They took their time, eating the flesh off a severed leg, picking intestines out of their teeth after taking a bite out of someone's torso, scratching their ass with a severed arm. By the time a hoard of the creatures reached Janine's co-worker Matilda's apartment building, Janine had run in, woken up Matilda's roommate, Thomas, grabbed her bugout bag, grabbed his keys, piled his still-half-asleep ass into the car and taken off with both men for Price Chopper to get Matilda.

~

Janine woke up clutching the photograph. She climbed out of her bunk, stretched all four limbs two by two, yawned, and farted. She wandered into the kitchen, to see if they still had any coffee. Nope, just some stale black tea. Janine set a pot of water to boil and sat at the table, reminiscing again of the past.

Matilda had insisted on going down to Western Mass to check on her parents. She took her car, so Janine, Bobby and Thomas took his car, and headed across the river to Madame Sherri's Forest. It was the only place they could think of on short notice, where they didn't think the aliens would swarm. They spent a chilly two nights hiding under the ruins of Madame Sherri's castle, surviving off of protein bars and water. On the third day, they ventured out to the nearby pond to try out the fishing line in Janine's bugout bag. They caught nothing.

"This isn't sustainable, we need to figure out what we're going to do," Thomas said morosely, as he chewed on another protein bar.

"I wish I didn't live so close to where the ships landed. We could get food, clothes, and guns at my house," Bobby lamented, again, for about the thousandth time.

Janine pulled a small, hand-cranked radio out of her bag. "Let's see if anyone is still alive out there." She cranked the radio, then turned it on and scanned the dial.

After heavy static for several turns of the dial, Janine thought she heard a snippet of a voice. She slowly turned the dial back, until the voice came into focus.

"…Keene, NH. I don't know how long until they find me in here. The doors are all locked, but I'm out of food and all I have is the water from the tap in the bathroom. I'll tell my story again. My name is John Thander. I'm a DJ here at KQAB. I was on the air when the ship touched down and crushed four blocks of downtown Keene. The aliens, oh gahd, they were horrible. I went out when I heard the crashing. The doors opened on the ship and the giant insects poured out. Oh my gahd they were horrible. They look like insects, but with a snout like a big dog, like a werewolf. Gahd bless you if you haven't encountered one of these creatures. They just, they just slaughtered. I ran back to the radio station and locked myself in. Some people followed me but I wouldn't let them in. I only had so much food…I'm sorry…

"As I stood by the door saying I was sorry through the window, one of those creatures came up behind the woman at the door and just, impaled her with its fingers, right through her neck. I watched as it squeezed out her eyeballs and ate them. It didn't just eat them. It savored them, like caviar. I couldn't move, but somehow the thing didn't see me, it just walked off. I know they'll be back, they've killed everyone. When the military finally showed up, their weapons did nothing. These things can take a bazooka blast and just get up and keep killing. They killed all of the soldiers. They're going to kill me. I'm getting so very hungry…"

The station faded out into static. Janine cranked the radio again and turned up and down the dial on AM and FM, but no more voices broke through.

"Let's venture out to Route 9, and see what we can see," said Thomas.

"I'm not sure that's a great idea, those things have got to be everywhere by now," Bobby cautioned.

"We can go when it gets dark, no headlights. I want to check out my studio on Old Ferry Road. You know, the one I set up in that old warehouse down the end of the street. I had a little bit of food there, mostly canned goods. There's a kitchen with a few pots and pans, too. We could have a hot meal and not have to take turns crouching in the dark under Madame Sherri's for another night."

"Alright, let's try some more fishing while we wait for dark." Janine repacked her bag and set off up the trail to the pond. Thomas and Bobby followed closely.

They got very lucky that night. They drove to the

warehouse just minutes before an alien patrol came down Putney Road, carrying weapons and large sacks in which to throw any human stragglers they came across.

The coast was clear at the warehouse. None of the other renters had made it there, it seemed. Thomas whipped up some rice and beans in the kitchen while Janine checked the radio again.

"Any luck?" asked Bobby.

"Nothing. I'll keep checking periodically. We should see whether there's anything left to loot at Hannaford and Aldi tomorrow night." Janine gave up turning the dial.

"Will do, but you know, I think there's an old CB radio in here, from when this place was a functional warehouse. You should check it out and see if there are any other survivors with one, or at least let anyone listening know we're here," said Thomas as he dished out three bowls and brought them to the table.

"CB? Wow, I haven't seen one of those since I was a kid. My dad was a trucker. I only saw him once in a while, but he'd let me play on the radio in his rig when he was visiting. He's why I had that bugout bag in the first place. He was always going on about being ready to run at any second, you never knew what could happen…" Janine reminisced. "I could live without those protein bars ever again. This is good. Thank you."

"Well I was talking to Bobby, seeing as he's the

police officer, but this is good that you know how to use one, too!" laughed Thomas.

"Well excuse me," Janine laughed.

~

Janine popped out of her reverie when Henry walked into the kitchen, poured himself a cup of tea, and sat down next to her.

"Hey where's mine?"

Henry grudgingly slid the first cup over and got up to prepare another. "So I hear we set us up the bomb."

"Speak English, Henry, please."

"I mean, we're going to be bombing the shit out of the Brattleboro slaughterhouses soon! I can't wait to get those bastards!"

"How soon? I hadn't heard anything more on Kalinda's progress."

"Sunday night, if I overheard Christian and Molly correctly."

"Sunday night??? We need more time to finalize our plan! Is Thomas awake yet?" Janine took a sip of her tea, then got up and stormed off toward the bunks.

"Whoa, someone's touchy about not being the first informed all the time." Henry sat back down at the table and sipped his tea.

Christian burst into the kitchen, wiping his

shoulder-length, dirty-blond hair out of his eyes. "We've got company!"

Henry jumped up, knocking the table and dumping his tea on his crotch. "Ah fuck! Ah FUCK! How many are there?" He leapt for the kitchen counter, whipped open a drawer, pulling it out too far and spilling its contents all over the floor.

"Whoa chill, dude! It's not the damn bugs," laughed Christian as his sister Molly and a strange, bedraggled woman wrapped in a blanket walked in. She was young, maybe early twenties, with green eyes and greasy, matted, curly brown hair. A plastic tag, embossed with a pattern of dots like Braille, hung from her right ear.

Molly stood with her arm around the new woman. "Haha Henry, dude, did you piss your pants thinkin' we were gettin' attacked?" Molly was almost literally a female version of Christian. They were twins. Molly's matching hair hung down to her mid back, but she had it pulled back into a no-nonsense ponytail. She spoke with the same hippie lilt as her brother. "This is Emily. She escaped a dairy farm in Keene."

"H-h-hi," squeaked Emily timidly.

Henry dropped the knife he had picked up off the floor and walked awkwardly over to Molly and Emily. "Hi, I'm Henry. I spilled tea on myself, I did not wet myself, I swear." He practically batted his bright brown eyes.

Emily giggled.

Henry sniffed. "Oh. I'm sure you're going to be wanting a bath." He stepped back and ran a hand nervously through his short, brown, frat-boy-cut hair.

Molly slapped Henry on the arm. "Not until we get some hot food in her. Would you make some tea, Christian?"

"Certainly, mein uh, sister." He started filling the pot with water. "Henry are you going to pick up those utensils, dude?"

Henry stared at Emily for a few more moments. "So how long were you there? How bad was it? What did they do to you?"

Molly had walked over to help Christian with the tea, but she turned and shot a look at him. "Henry, jeez would you stop grilling her before she even gets a chance to sit down?" She walked back over to Emily and guided her to a chair at the table. "You could have, you know, been more of a gentleman and helped her sit down."

Henry blushed. "I'm sorry, I, uh…" He looked at the floor and shuffled over to clean up the drawer contents he had spilled in his panic.

Janine and Thomas walked into the kitchen.

"Whoa, it's crowded in here. Where's Kalinda? … Oh, who's this?" Thomas rushed over to Emily and extended his hand. "Thomas, and this is my trusty sidekick, Janine. You look like you've been through hell and back! Who is making this poor girl some tea?"

"Coming right up!" Christian brought a steaming mug to the table and slid it in front of Emily.

Emily stood slowly and timidly shook Thomas' hand. "I'm Emily. I ran away from a dairy farm in Keene. I'm, I'm sorry, I've been running for six hours…"

Thomas extended his arm. "Please, please sit! What do we have on the menu for our honored guest?"

"Cream of Wheat, shelf-stable bacon, and tofu scramble. I'm afraid there's no such thing as eggs anymore. We got what was salvageable from Hannaford and what we could find in local houses." Molly went back to stirring two pans on the stove, while Christian cut open a shrink-wrapped package of cooked bacon and laid the strips out on a cookie sheet to heat in the oven.

"Going all out! Good! You've been through a harrowing ordeal, you must tell me all about how you escaped. I'll open a bottle of wine after you've gotten a bath and some rest. Ah, here's a fine meal. Enjoy, my dear." Thomas stepped to the side as Molly placed a plate in front of Emily.

"I, I don't think I can eat bacon, after what they did to me…They were, they are farming us! Just like we're cows! Slaughtering us like we're pigs! They, they, they made me pregnant… I'm pregnant! I can't be pregnant!" Emily burst into sobs and put her head in her hands.

"Okay, okay, I'll take the bacon!" Henry pulled the four strips off her plate and stuffed them into his mouth, one by one.

Emily calmed down enough to take a few bites of tofu. "This is actually good," she sniffled.

"What do you think they did with all the cows?" Henry finished chewing and swallowed. "I mean, they musta took them somewhere. You think they just killed them all?"

Christian looked timidly at Emily, then shot a harsh look at Christian. "Dude, really? Thomas said they shipped them off somewhere else to farm them, too, just like we farmed them. They're just farming everything and everyone."

Molly saw that Emily had finished, and took her plate. "Seconds?"

"Yes please," sniffed Emily. "They fed us nothing but grain mush, out of a trough. We had to eat with our hands, it feels so good to see a fork again..." She started sobbing again.

Henry brought Emily a fresh cup of tea. "There, there, you're safe here now." He put a hand on her shoulder. "We're going to bring those fuckers down. Don't you worry."

"How?" gasped Emily finally, after a hiccupping sob.

"We've got our very own ex-military bomb

specialist, Kalinda. You'll meet her later." Thomas sat down across from Emily. Janine sat down next to her.

"Guys, could we have a moment with Emily?" Thomas asked the room.

Molly nodded her head as she gently placed another plate of food in front of Emily. She joined Christian and they walked out together. Henry gave Emily another squeeze on her shoulder and followed.

"This might be hard to talk about, but you need to decide what you want to do about your pregnancy," Thomas said gently.

"I want it gone! I want it out of me!" Emily shoved the plate of food away. "I'm not hungry anymore." She sobbed once, then choked back another. "Is there really anything you can do?"

Janine spoke up. "How far along are you?"

"They tied me to the rape rack nine weeks ago."

"Rape rack?" Janine looked shocked.

"That's what we called it, us girls. Oh gahd, the other girls. I couldn't take anyone with me, I had to run when I could. I wish I could have taken them with me! Oh gahd!" Emily broke into sobs again.

"You did what you could under the circumstances." Janine put a hand on Emily's.

"The good news, Emily, is that we raided a few local pharmacies two weeks ago," said Thomas. "We have pills you can take that will end your pregnancy, if that's what you really…"

"I want this thing out of me!" Emily cried.

"Okay. It's going to be painful, it's basically going to cause a miscarriage. We have oxycodone or hydrocodone you could take for the pain."

"As long as it gets this thing out of me." Emily took a deep breath. "Could I possibly bathe and get some clothes now?"

"Of course. We still have hot water as long as the propane holds out. I'll see what I can find that will fit you." Janine led Emily out of the kitchen, toward the private bathroom in the office section of the warehouse.

Thomas sat down at the table and looked around at the kitchen.

"The main room is coming along nicely. We'll be able to start renting out studio spaces within the next few weeks." Victor's voice echoed through Thomas' head. He had stood behind Thomas as he sat at the table, with a cup of tea in one hand and his other on his partner's shoulder. "That should pay the mortgage. We can start converting the upstairs offices to a gallery space, and there's ample room in the back area to bring in some bunks so people can even crash here if they're really into a project…"

Thomas stood and turned to Victor. "This has always been my dream, this artist community, and here we are, building it. I love you so much." He leaned in and kissed Victor sweetly. "Thank you so much, my love."

"You know I wanted this as much as you as soon

as you told me about it. There's nothing else I'd rather do with that money than make you happy." Victor had secured the warehouse with a modest inheritance sum.

Thomas smiled. A tear leaked from the inner corner of his eye, then dropped to the table. He sighed. Victor had been killed when the first ship had touched down right on top of the People's Bank he worked at on the day it arrived.

He stood and walked out of the kitchen towards his own studio space. Once there he picked up his sketch of Victor. He had captured the sharp jawline, his piercing green eyes, the business casual haircut, his full, Taurus lips. Thomas sighed and looked toward the corner, at a painting he had been working on the day Victor asked him to move in with him.

"I can't just abandon Matilda, she's been my friend since college." Thomas dipped his brush in the paint and added a white line along the stem of a single flower, being held by a little girl, who stood in front of an apocalyptic hellscape.

"You wouldn't be abandoning her, she'd have plenty of time to find a new roommate."

"You don't understand, she's my best friend. Other than you, of course, love. She and I've been roommates for twenty years!"

Victor had pulled over a chair and sat down on it backwards, facing Thomas. "I understand you don't like change, I mean you're a Taurus too after all, but

I love you, Tom, and I think it's about time we gave it a try."

Thomas had sighed and pushed away the easel, and draped his palette and brushes onto his desk. "I told you, I'll think about it. I'm just not sure it's not…"

"Too soon? I've been your boyfriend for two years. How long is long enough? I'm getting tired of waiting for you to stop being afraid!" Victor stood and walked toward the door of the studio. He stopped and looked at Thomas. "Honestly, Tom, I'm not sure I can wait much longer. You need to decide, me or Matilda." He walked out of the room, slamming the door.

That had been the last time he had seen Victor. The aliens had touched down two days later. Thomas had spent the entire week afterwards in bed, only getting up to use the bathroom or force himself to eat something. The day Janine dragged him out of bed and into the car, he had been contemplating suicide, again.

Now he looked again at the sketch of Victor. He picked up a thumbtack and stuck the picture to the wall above his desk. He sighed. "I'm going to keep fighting. For you, for Matilda, for everyone. This isn't the end of the world, Goddamnit." He turned off the light and went back to the kitchen.

~

Kalinda finished soldering the second to last wire to the timer on the pipe bomb she was assembling. She liked to wait to solder the last wire on all of them until the day before they were going to be used. Just in case anyone decided to become a martyr like Arturo. He had hatched a plan to strap a few to himself and try to run into a slaughterhouse. Kalinda still didn't understand what he thought he was going to accomplish. The aliens could withstand bombs. He was more likely to kill humans. That was two weeks ago. All he had managed to do was start cutting through the fence with bolt cutters, when it started raining. He kept working through it as the rain got heavier and heavier. Pretty quickly, he was soaked. So were the bombs. Kalinda hadn't weatherproofed them. The timer sparked on one of the six he had strapped to himself, setting off the fuse, setting off the bomb, setting off the other five bombs, and well, there wasn't much of Arturo left to bury. He did blow a nice hole in the fence. The bugs had it patched within the day.

Henry had made a crack that Arturo must have converted to Islam at the last second. No one laughed. Janine had told him to shut the fuck up.

Good ol' Janine. She was a strong kid. Kalinda probably would have had a raging crush on her if she weren't so young.

After twelve years in the Army working in

ordinance disposal, Kalinda had retired and gone to bartending school. She had worked as a bartender for ten years, then had enough of that and bought a motorcycle. She had saved up enough to take the summer off and road trip through the U.S. She was packing the day the first ship touched down. She got a call from her friend Sherry, who asked if she should cancel the going away party she had been planning. Kalinda said nothing would stop her from this road trip. She ventured downtown out of curiosity a few times during the next week, but nothing ever happened with the spaceship.

The morning the invasion took place, Kalinda was still asleep with a hangover. She had planned to leave that afternoon. She was awakened by the sound of her next-door neighbor screaming through the wall. There was a huge thump against the wall and the screaming stopped. Kalinda jumped out of bed and grabbed her gun from the nightstand. She ran out the back door, to the balcony she shared with that neighbor. She peeked through the window and gasped. A giant bug with a wolf's snout was munching on her neighbor. Kalinda leaned back against the wall next to the window and took a deep breath. "This can't be real," she said under her breath. "Someone slipped something into one of my drinks last night." She peeked in the window a second time to see the bug's ass end exiting the room, and the remains of her neighbor spread over the floor.

She went back to her apartment and peeked out the window by the front door. Another giant bug was clambering toward her door. She ran back to her bedroom and back out onto the balcony. The courtyard was empty. She looked down at the two-story drop, then sucked in a breath and tried the door handle to her neighbor's apartment. It was unlocked. Kalinda heard her own front door crash open as she slipped in the door quietly and shut it behind her. She slipped through the bedroom without looking too long at the remains of her neighbor and went toward the front hall. The front door stood open, the lock smashed. Kalinda went into the second bedroom. It was empty. Bangs and screams sounded from upstairs and the next adjoining apartment. The closet had been emptied, presumably by the bugs looking for more victims. She kicked aside a pile of clothing, sat down in the closet, and pulled the door closed. She sat in the dark, clutching at her gun, for what seemed like hours.

When she finally had come out and returned to her apartment, it had also been ransacked. No possible hiding place had been ignored. Kalinda found her trip bag and dumped the contents on her bed. She pulled out the nightstand drawer and dumped all the ammo she had into the bag. She repacked her tent and a few other items and went into the kitchen to grab some food.

When she saw that the coast was clear, she went

down to get her motorcycle. At the last second she changed her mind. The noise would attract attention. She got off her bike and started hiking east, to look for other survivors.

Kalinda snapped out of her reverie, put down the soldering iron and walked out of her shop toward the kitchen. She pulled her long, black hair out of its ponytail and shook her head as she walked. She could go for a cup of tea and whatever she could whip up as quickly as possible, probably pasta and beans.

Thomas was washing dishes when Kalinda walked in. "Ah! Just the person I wanted to see!"

"Hi Thomas. You probably want a status report? I'll trade you for a pot of water for tea."

Thomas filled the pan and handed it to Kalinda. "How goes the arts and crafts? Are we on schedule?"

"Everything is ship-shape, sarge." Kalinda mockingly saluted Thomas. "I'll just need a few hours to finish the soldering before we're good to go. Is it still on for Sunday night?"

"I'm thinking of postponing. We got a guest today. A woman who escaped from a dairy farm in Keene. I'd like to give her a bit of time to acclimate to life here before we go gallivanting off all over Brattleboro with a bunch of bombs."

"Oh? She escaped from a dairy farm? How in the hell did she manage to do that?"

"I've yet to hear her story. I'm thinking of opening some of our oh-so-valuable bottles of wine tonight and getting to know her. Everyone is welcome." Thomas rinsed the last dish and put it in the strainer. "There's leftover tofu scramble in that bowl in the fridge. Molly made a ton of it. It's fantastic."

"Sounds good. I'm so psyched we still have electricity. It's like the bugs just ignored the grid in the places they didn't do any construction." Kalinda pulled the bowl out of the fridge. "I feel like I could eat all of this."

"They must not have seen our electrical system as a threat. I'm amazed there were no interruptions to Old Ferry Road, though. Grateful, but amazed. It could go out any time, of course, but we're living in a post-apocalyptic lap of luxury right now. Oh your tea water is ready, I'll get it for you."

Kalinda laughed. "Lap of luxury indeed!" She wiped her black hair out of her eyes with one hand as she placed the bowl in the microwave. "We've even got microwave popcorn!" She lifted the box on top of the microwave and waved it back and forth.

~

"We raided the clothing store on Putney Road in the first few days. There should be at least a few things that will fit you." Janine handed Emily a clean blanket to wrap herself in and led her down a short hallway to the combination pantry and supply room. "These garbage bags here. Take your time. I'll wait out at the pantry entrance."

"Thank you." Emily picked up the first bag and brought it over to a small table.

Janine closed the pantry door and sat on a stack of cases of canned goods in the hallway.

Fifteen minutes later, Emily emerged in a pink sweat suit, carrying a small stack of clothing. "These all fit me. This is n-n-not exactly my style, but beggars can't be choosers, right?"

"You're not a beggar, you're a survivor." Janine stood and stretched. "Let's drop those in your bunk and get down to the lounge."

"Lounge?"

"Well, it's really just a huge room with a bunch of couches in a circle. This place was some kind of hippie dippy art commune before the invasion."

"Yeah, sounds nice." Emily distractedly stared around at the art on the hallway walls. "This place is real nice. You guys have it real nice."

"You do too, now." Janine opened the door to the stairwell. "We're a small family here. You'll fit right in."

Janine and Emily walked out of the stairwell into a cavernous room. It was huge enough that walls had been constructed all around the perimeter and the area divided into rooms, most of which were studios. Christmas lights were strung between columns over the rest of the room, creating a spotted grid that floated about ten feet in the air above the "lounge". Couches of several different colors were arranged in a circle, each with a coffee table in front, and end tables with lamps on the side. The couches were draped with afghans of a rainbow of colors, and contrasting, squishy throw pillows congested the corners of each sofa. A patchwork of area rugs of various sizes covered the floor. To the left of the couch circle was a TV area, tables with mismatched chairs and a few more couches were scattered about to the right.

Thomas, Henry, Molly, Christian, and five other people Emily had not met were seated on the couches.

"Ah, there's our guest of honor!" Thomas stood and picked up a glass of wine which he held out toward Emily.

"I… I didn't realize there were so many of you!" Emily stuttered as she took the wine.

"Emily you've met Molly, Christian, and, erm, Henry…"

Henry snickered then piped up, "Hi Em!"

Thomas continued, "This beauty next to me is Kalinda, to my left are Jimbo, Pixie, Shawn, and Gibson. Not pictured are Bobby and Jenny, who are still recovering from a terrible accident, and Lucy and Dave, who are on watch at the north and south entrances, respectively."

"It… It's nice to meet you all."

"Please, have a seat." Thomas gestured to the couch to his right.

Janine and Emily sat. Janine poured herself a glass of wine.

"We're all here because we'd like to hear your story, if you're willing to share with us." Thomas began. "We'll all share our stories with you, too, if the night is long enough. Some of them are more, er, interesting than others…"

"Th-th-that's fine." Emily took a sip of wine, and then a gulp. "I was a waitress, here in Brattleboro. Place on Main Street called Echo. I lived down on Frost Place, you know, where that weird, abandoned church was. A-a-anyway, I had the day off the day the first ship came. I was asleep and one of my roommates ran in screaming about a giant space ship crushing downtown from Main Street back to School Street. Frost Street was blocked at Elm Street so we ran down Canal Street to see. I might have saw you in the crowd in the days after that, Janine. I certainly remember your red hair. I-I-I remember cracking a joke about the ship barely missing my work.

"I wasn't there yet that day when the second ship arrived and they opened up. I was actually walking toward downtown, I was by the crack houses on Canal Street, when people started screaming and running back past me. Someone said they were killing people, to run. I didn't make it back to my house before one of the things grabbed me from behind and threw me in a giant sack with other people. We could b-b-barely breathe, all squashed together and bumping around as we felt the thing walking along. After what seemed like forever, we were dumped out into a transport ship, and brought up to the Common where we were stuffed into a corral. The next day they separated men and women. Th-th-they were just picking us up and ripping off our clothes to see! A few people broke a leg or an arm when they tossed us in the corral. Everyone was just screaming and crying, it was so chaotic. We were all, us women were, s-s-sc-scanned by some sort of thing on our stomachs. Some women were thrown on one ship, some women on another. The one they put me on ended up going to the dairy farm in Keene. They threw already pregnant women in with us.

"At the farm they tagged our ears and we were scanned again, and they, and they…" Emily hiccupped. "They probed us, down there. The girls thought they were figuring out when we were going to ovulate. That's when they tied us to the rape rack. They, they inseminated us! They tied me down spread eagle, and stuck a finger in my asshole. It hurt, it burned so badly. They poked around for my uterus then stuck a baster-looking thing in my vagina and squirted me full, of, somebody. Oh gahd I don't even know who the father might be! They scanned us and raped us again every day until they seemed to be satisfied that it had worked, then they took us to another floor. There were all the very pregnant women there. They had machines on them, pumping their breast milk." Emily started sobbing.

"Take your time, sweetie." Janine gently rubbed Emily's back and poured her another glass of wine.

"Th-thank you." Emily sipped and continued. "Last night I saw a chance to escape, and I took it. It was shift change with the aliens. Apparently the next shift was late. All but two of the aliens left. When they weren't looking I climbed the fence and just ran. I recognized Route 9 and ran and ran. If I saw anything coming I hid in the trees on the side of the road until they passed. The only thing I could think to do was get back to Brattleboro. When I crossed the bridge I ran into Christian and Molly out to loot houses, and well, you know the rest."

Everyone just sat in stunned silence for a few minutes. Emily sipped her wine nervously.

Shawn was the first to speak up. "I escaped from the Brattleboro Retreat four weeks ago. Well, what used to be the Retreat. I was sorted into it on the first day. They turned the Retreat into a breeding facility. I was crammed into one room with six other guys. Three times a day they took us out, lined us up, and shocked our testicles to force us to ejaculate. They collected it to… Oh gahd. You could be carrying my baby, for all I know…"

"They keep women at the Retreat, also, it's a massive breeding operation to breed us for slaughter and dairy farms. They've built a massive feedlot facility on the remainder of the Retreat property. Babies and children are crammed into cages in massive sheds. They seem to be sending adults to slaughter as soon as they catch them."

"How do you know all this, Thomas?" asked Henry.

"I've observed, Henry. It would behoove you to do some of that some of the time."

"Behoove! Listen to Mr. Vocabulary star over here, folks."

"Henry, don't get started. This is not the occasion." said Janine sharply.

"Fine, just trying to lighten things up a bit…" Henry scowled into his wine glass.

"It would behoove us to obtain more of this wine, methinks." Thomas got up and disappeared into the stairwell.

Janine took Emily's hand. "Gibson is a doctor, he'll be overseeing your abortion, making sure everything goes smoothly."

Emily looked at Gibson. "Thank you."

"You're welcome, my dear." Gibson peered at Emily over his glasses. "You seem to be in ship shape, you should get through this just fine. I can remove that tag from your ear for you, also."

Thomas returned with three more bottles of wine, a bong, and a huge bag of weed. "I've been growing this stuff, right here in the basement, since before it was legal in Vermont! Haha! Alright, let's get this party started!"

Janine guffawed and Emily giggled.

~

"Citizens On Patrol! Chug-ug-ug-ug-ug-ug…" Kalinda did a bad impression of the guy from the *Police Academy* movies who could sound like a helicopter, among other things.

Janine laughed. "I'll have to see those movies someday. I'm too young. I was born in '97."

"Ah that's when I bloody graduated high school! You're just old enough to drink legally!" Kalinda exclaimed. She stopped at a tree stump and put her leg up on it, resting the butt of her rifle on her knee. "I remember seeing those movies when I was a little kid. I loved them so much. We'll have to watch them sometime when we rebuild after this apocalypse."

"I've been drinking since I was fifteen, the aliens didn't ruin anything for me." Janine pulled a bag of beef jerky out of her pack. "Do you think they make human jerky? The aliens?"

"That's gross. I'm not sure I can eat meat any more, after this. The way they farm us, just like we farmed animals… It made me think a lot."

"You have a point." Janine pulled a piece out of the bag and stuck it in her mouth. "Maybe I'll stop eating meat after this is over with. Want some?"

Kalinda sighed and reached for the bag. "I wish we… Shit, hear that?" She took her leg down.

"Bugs!" Janine stage whispered. "Trees! Over there!"

The women ran to two thick, older trees and climbed them as quickly as they could to about sixteen feet up. Kalinda unslung her pack and pulled out the net. She flung one end to Janine, and they held it out, ready to drop it if one of the bugs came in range.

Two bugs carrying weapons but no sacks sauntered by about eight meters away from either of the women. After the bugs had passed to a safe distance, Janine tossed her end of the net back to Kalinda, who stuffed it back into her pack. They climbed down.

"They didn't have sacks, I guess they're not looking to capture us alive anymore," Kalinda said.

"I think that might be better than going through what poor Emily's been through," Janine replied.

"That's very nihilistic of you." Kalinda poked her in the arm. They continued on their patrol. "So, there was this guy called Bobcat Goldthwaite…"

There was a quick sizzling sound and a puff of dirt at their feet. They turned and ran behind more trees.

"Shit! Shit! They turned around! They saw us! How the hell did they see us? How the hell did they aim?" Janine said in a panicked whisper.

Kalinda dropped to the ground with her rifle and peered around the tree. "Can you climb that tree?" She pointed.

"Yes."

"Take the net." Kalinda shimmied back up against her tree and out of her pack and handed it to Janine. She picked up a few acorns and threw them hard to the left. The bugs stopped and fired in that direction.

Janine quickly took off her pack and put on Kalinda's, then climbed the tree. Kalinda stood up, bent over, and picked up a few more acorns.

When Janine was sixteen feet up, Kalinda cocked her rifle and tossed an acorn a little closer to their hiding place. Puffs of dirt flew up and a sizzling sound filled the air for a second. Kalinda waited, peeked quickly around the tree to make sure the bugs had moved closer, then tossed another acorn, just two meters from the bottom of Janine's tree. She waited for the bugs to shoot and then move in that direction, then tossed the last acorn right at the bugs.

"Now!" Kalinda shouted.

The net came flying down and caught one of the bugs. It flailed and got tangled, but still had its finger on the trigger of its weapon. The sizzling sound crackled against the net. Suddenly the bug was shaking instead of flailing.

The other bug tried to pull the net off and got shocked, causing it to fly onto its back, stunned.

Kalinda from partway behind her tree, and Janine from her branch, watched as the tangled bug started to smoke. A whistling sound came from its exoskeleton as its guts started boiling. Neon-yellow goo began bubbling from the creature's mouth, hissing and turning black as it dribbled down its jawline and neck before it dripped to the ground.

Finally the bug's finger was too burned to hold the trigger down any more and the sizzling stopped. The neon-yellow goo steamed and abated to a slow drip. The arms and antennae of the creature fractured, then crumbled with a crackling noise.

Janine started to climb down from the tree. Kalinda grabbed the bolt cutters in one hand from Janine's discarded pack and began to walk toward the stunned bug with her rifle in the other. Just as she leaned in to try to see if it was still alive, it woke up.

The bug's arm whipped around and grabbed the arm that was holding the bolt cutters. She dropped them and tried to pull away as another alien hand grabbed her opposite leg and began to pull. Kalinda screamed in pain. She reached back and aimed the rifle like a spear, and drove it into the soft flesh in one of the bug's armpits. Neon-yellow blood spurted all over the gun and Kalinda's hand. The creature dropped her other arm and she flung it at the rifle butt and hung on with both hands as the bug grabbed her by the head and pulled. Kalinda screamed again and it cut off to a gargle as a wet ripping sound reached Janine's ears and Kalinda's head came off. Red blood splattered and mixed with neon yellow on the ground like a Jackson Pollock. The bug dropped Kalinda and her head.

Janine jumped down from the tree and ran screaming at the hideous, blood-spattered creature. It turned to grab her. She leaped at the rifle, and grabbed onto it as the bug took hold of her by the torso. She quickly found the trigger and fired. The bug's blood splattered out all over Janine as the bug let her go and she fell to the ground on top of Kalinda. She rolled off and ran about five meters before turning around.

The bug pulled the rifle out of its armpit and started walking toward Janine. Blood gushed from its armpit and mouth. It fell to the ground reaching for Janine about a meter from her and didn't get up.

~

Thomas did his best to soothe Janine. "Kalinda was a hard worker and she would be so proud of everything you've done, and will do. She fought hard to the last second. We're all going to miss her so much."

Janine stared at a painting in the lounge that she hadn't noticed until now. It was an alien, not like these bugs, this was a typical big-eyed grey, the kind that was basically iconic. It held the Earth in one hand,

and made a peace sign with the other. It was very ironic. Janine wanted to tear it to shreds.

Thomas continued, "Janine, we're all so proud of the two of you for taking down that pair of bugs. Not everyone could have done what you did."

"Anyone would have done what I did under the circumstances. Kalinda was the brave one. I can't get the image out of my head of that motherfucker tearing her head off. It just keeps repeating…"

"That's normal for a traumatic experience. Just let me know if there's anything I can do for you, anything at all." Thomas put his hand on Janine's shoulder.

"I actually could use one of those bottles of wine you have stashed in the basement."

"Coming right up." Thomas stood and disappeared into the stairwell.

Janine looked at the awful painting again. She decided the alien was mocking her. She stood and walked over, took it down, and returned to the couch.

"What we expected versus what we got, huh?" Thomas said as he returned. He opened the bottle of wine he had retrieved and produced two clean glasses. Pouring the wine, he said, "My friend Kenneth painted that as a joke about the state of the nation back in 2016. He said 'It's a cry for help. We need these guys to save us from ourselves.' Do you think they've saved us from ourselves, Janine?"

Janine stared at the painting for another thirty

seconds before answering. "Well if you consider how things were going with global warming and this country… No, they certainly didn't save us, but maybe they saved the Earth from us."

"I heard on the radio this morning from Greenfield. They were relaying a message from North Carolina. The bugs seem to have started mining. They seem to be here to eke every last resource out of the planet." Thomas sipped his wine. "It's very strange, wondering how long they observed us before they invaded. Are they responsible for all of the flying saucer sightings over the years?

"Oh, I almost forgot!" Thomas pulled a bag of weed out of his pocket. "I just finished curing this today. It's strawberry cough." He picked a pre-rolled joint out of the bag and lit it. "Try that, and then cough."

"Tastes like strawberries, I know, I've seen *Children of Men*." Janine took a puff.

"That movie inspired me to grow this." Thomas laughed.

Just then, Henry and Christian came jogging into the room from the stairwell.

"There you are! Christian found Kalinda's notes. We can finish the bombs without blowing ourselves up!" said Henry excitedly.

"Henry, dude, that's…" Christian started to scold.

"Too soon? Come on, Kalinda would want us to

soldier on, don't you think?" Henry dropped a notebook on the coffee table in front of Thomas.

"Thank you guys, but now's not the best time." Thomas gestured at Janine.

"I'm fine, really," said Janine, "Henry's right, Kalinda would want us to stick to the plan." She took another hit from the joint she was still holding and held it up to Henry. "It's strawberry cough."

Henry took a hit and passed it on to Christian. "Pull my finger!" he said with a Michael Caine accent.

Janine laughed at the movie reference and picked up her glass of wine. She decided that tomorrow she would finish the bombs for Kalinda. She picked up the painting she had placed to the side and looked at it one more time. She pulled a lighter from her pocket and looked at Thomas. "May I?"

"Yes, please, I hate that piece of shit."

~

"Okay, the timers on your first bombs are set for fifteen minutes, and the second for ten. Don't mix them up. Let's sync our watches, and plan on hitting the on switches on the first ones at 11:30, and the second at 11:35. That'll give us ten minutes to get as far away as possible. They've usually shut down for the night by eleven, so we shouldn't have to worry about getting any people out of there first." Janine unfolded a map of Brattleboro on the kitchen table.

"Pixie, Jimbo, and Lucy, you three will take the facility down on Route 142 by the river. Henry, Molly, and Shawn, you've got the Canal Street slaughterhouse. You six should take the Mountain Road trail on the New Hampshire side of the river, to the south bridge. That way you can avoid Main Street. Christian, Thomas and I will take out the Putney Road facility. Just get in there, place your bombs, press the buttons, and get out."

"Sounds good, I just, don't know if I can do this." Pixie, usually very quiet, spoke up. She clutched Jimbo's hand so tightly her knuckles were white. Her short, spiky blond hair was usually more pale than her skin, but not right at this moment.

"You're strong, love, we'll get through this, nothing is gonna go wrong." Jimbo kissed Pixie on the cheek.

"Not as long as we play our cards right and get really, really lucky." Henry poked Thomas on the arm. "Hey boss I'm pretty nervous, how about being a little less stingy with that strawberry cough?"

Thomas laughed and handed Henry a joint. "I've got one for anyone else who needs one, too."

"I'll take one," said Gibson.

"You're not even going, dude!" Christian took one from the pile in front of Thomas.

"Someone has to hold down the fort." Thomas handed Gibson a joint.

"Alright everyone, party it up now, we've got six

hours 'til we have to head out." Janine turned to Emily. "Did Thomas show you how to man the radio? At midnight we'd like you to make an announcement on the air that Brattleboro has begun the fight. Say some inspiring stuff about how you overcame what you went through, survivors like us eat that stuff up."

Emily laughed. "I-I-I'll do my best."

Six hours later, nine mountain bikes and nine backpacks were lined up outside the south entrance to the warehouse.

"Remember, just get in there, hit the switches, and get out. No heroics," Janine told everyone. "Good luck."

"We're gonna need it." Henry took one last puff off a roach and tossed it to the side. "Could, could I actually have a hug? From everybody?"

Two teams rode off west down Old Ferry Road. Janine, Thomas, and Christian didn't have as far to ride, so they waited a bit before heading out. After one more round of hugs with Emily and Gibson, the three mounted their bicycles and took off the same way as the others. When they reached the roundabout on Putney Road, a huge shadow appeared in the sky to the east.

"It's moving toward us! Lights off! Get to the underpass!" Thomas gently shouted. They veered right off the roundabout and stopped under the remnants of the old Highway 91 underpass. All three climbed off their bikes and huddled behind a couch-sized chunk of fallen concrete. They watched as the black, shadowy hulk of the transport ship veered south over the trees after crossing the river.

"Is that heading to one of the South Bratt slaughterhouses? Did they not close down for the night?" Janine whispered nervously.

"It could be headed to the breeding facility, or just back to the main ship for the night, I don't know. I couldn't see if there were people on it. It's too dark," Thomas replied.

"Speaking of which, why the hell did you say lights off, the bugs are blind dude," Christian interjected.

"Because if there had been humans on that ship the bugs would have sensed them yelling at us for help," Thomas said dejectedly.

"That's cold, dude, we'd need to help people on that ship!"

"How, Christian? Tell me how." Thomas got up from behind the concrete and picked up his bike.

"Calm down, both of you. We've got a job to get done." Janine whipped an arm south toward the slaughterhouse. "We can only do what we can. We can't exactly shoot down a fucking bug ship."

"Let's get back onto Putney Road. We can argue about this later." Thomas gestured with his handlebars.

Janine and Christian walked to their bikes and

got on. "Be extra careful approaching the fence, we don't know if these fuckers are working or not," said Janine as she turned her headlamp back on.

They rode back out to the roundabout and headed south on Putney Road after making sure the coast was clear. The bugs had razed the shopping plaza a half mile down the road that had held a clothing store, Asian restaurant, office supply store, and a discount supermarket called Aldi. The facility they had built in its place was a monstrosity. Four stories of pure hell. The transport ships landed on the roof and people were herded slowly down a ramp that hugged the side of the fourth floor, to their deaths behind a door. A chain-link fence surrounded the roof's perimeter, and the ramp entirely, so any human thinking of jumping was prevented from escaping the more gruesome, terrifying death the bugs had planned for them.

No one could figure out why they closed down the place at night. The bugs didn't need light, so it didn't make any real sense. When sitting in the lounge shooting the shit they had come up with many theories, including sleep, or leisure time. Henry had suggested the bugs needed their sexy time and Janine had tossed a towel damp with spilled wine at his head. Thomas had insisted it was valid speculation because they did indeed have genitals, they were just hidden behind armored plates that must swing out of the way when they were aroused. Janine had walked over to Henry, picked up the towel, and flung it at Thomas.

As they approached the fence surrounding the former shopping plaza, they dismounted their bikes and left them lying on the side of the road by the old car dealership next door. They turned off their headlamps again and crept slowly to the fence.

"I don't see any movement, down here or on the roof," whispered Thomas. "Let's try a light." He switched on his headlamp and aimed it through the fence. The door at the far end of the building stood open. Nothing moved within. Thomas pulled a larger flashlight from his pack. "Alright, let's get in there and get this done."

Christian pulled bolt cutters from his pack and began cutting a hole in the fence. Janine and Thomas went over bomb placement.

"Don't worry about equipment, focus on knocking out the building's structure. Find columns that look load-bearing, and then put your second one somewhere on the perimeter. I'll head straight to the back, you two head right and split up at the middle." Thomas gestured skyward. "As tempting as it is to see what's on the upper floors, stay downstairs. Meet me back at the bikes."

Christian finished cutting a person-sized hole in the fence, and put the bolt cutters back in his pack. "Good luck you guys."

The three of them snuck through the fence and ran to the wall of the slaughterhouse, then walked quietly to the open door at the south end of the building. They still heard nothing, so Janine stuck her head around into the doorway. "Coast looks clear."

The first thing that hit them was the smell. Clotted blood, shit and disinfectant, and fear.

Thomas' large flashlight revealed walls of machinery, disappearing off into the distance both straight ahead and off to the right. Conveyor belts stretched between machinery like castle walls between hulking mechanical towers.

"This looks like a final processing and packing area on this floor. Those look like the shipping containers over there…"

"Thomas, it's 11:21. We don't really have time," Janine said nervously. "You said yourself…"

"I know, I'm sorry. I'll see you two soon." Thomas set off down the rows of machinery at the south end of the building.

Janine and Christian walked to what seemed about halfway along the east side, then Christian veered off to the left down the middle of the massive room. He had to climb under rows of conveyor belts to follow a row of columns roughly parallel to Thomas' path. Janine continued along until she came to a huge ramp leading upward. *Just a peek…* She glanced at her watch. *Damn.* She glanced longingly up the ramp, then trotted down the north end of the building until she came upon a row of thick columns about twenty feet apart that looked like they supported the floor above. She jogged in, counting five columns in, and unslung her pack. She pulled out the first of her two bombs, and a roll of duct tape, and strapped the bomb to the column. She glanced at her watch again. 11:28, two minutes to kill. She aimed her headlamp up and down the aisle she was standing in. It was so quiet she could hear Thomas or Christian walking elsewhere in the building. Tiny night sounds echoed through the cavernous room, between the machines and conveyor belts. Janine stared into the darkness down the aisle. For a moment, she felt, rather than saw, something rushing at her from the blackness, but she couldn't move. Seconds passed. Nothing appeared.

Janine jumped when her watch beeped. It was 11:30. She crouched and flipped the cover over the switch on the bomb and pressed the on button; *15:00* appeared on the LED screen in bright, red numbers. She pressed the start button and it began counting down. Janine took one last look down the aisle, then turned and trotted back toward the north wall and the ramp to the second floor. She duct taped her second bomb to the bottom of the ramp, nestled in the corner against the outer wall. At 11:35 she turned it on so it displayed *10:00*. She pressed start and jogged back toward the back door.

Thomas and Christian were waiting with the bikes. "That went off without a hitch!" said Thomas.

"Yeah, let's get the hell away from this place, it's

fucking with my head." Janine looked back at the massive, dark facility. She pictured transport ships coming in to land on the roof, then unloading their awful cargo. She saw bugs herding and shoving people down the ramp into the kill floor, where more bugs waited to knock them on the head then grab them by a leg and chain them up in a row, then on to the next bug, who slit their throat, and so on… Janine shuddered and mounted her bike.

The three rode north back to the underpass and waited for the explosion. After a few more minutes, a blast loud enough to shake the air concussed from the south. Thomas and Janine high-fived, and Christian jumped up with a whoop. "Awright!" he yelled.

"Let's get home and see how the others did," Thomas said gleefully.

~

Emily ran up to Janine with open arms. "It is ss-s-so good to see you guys! I've been freaking out!" She embraced Janine. "The others aren't back yet, just you three. I-I-I'm still worried, but it's so good to see you! I made the announcement on the radio, and I heard back from so many people! I can't believe there are so many others still out there! I talked to a lady in Florida, and a guy from Kansas for ten minutes or so, said he's the leader of a small resistance band down there. He called himself Lonesome Cowboy Bill. He was really nice. He said we gave them hope. Then…"

"Whoa, slow down girl! Did you hear anything from Liam in Keene?" asked Thomas.

"N-n-no, nothing from Keene." Emily hung her head.

"Damn!" Thomas swung a fist and looked at the sky. "Those were good people over there. I was hoping they'd have gotten some of your friends out of the dairy farm by now. Maybe there was just no one by the radio. We can only hope…"

"That's a huge bummer dude, I'm sorry." Christian patted Thomas on the shoulder.

Thirty minutes later, the others rode up.

"We should get the bikes and everybody inside. We spotted ships patrolling over Brattleboro the whole ride back up the trail," said Shawn as he swung off his bike.

"We expected that, yeah, let's get inside," said Janine. "I'll relieve Gibson at the north entrance for a while, would someone take this post?"

"Let me take a piss and I'll do it," said Henry, still breathing heavily from the bike ride. He went inside.

"Alright. I don't know about the rest of you, but I'm starving. How about I whip up some rice and beans?" asked Molly.

"I'll help you, sister dear." Christian followed Molly in.

"I just want to get some sleep," said Shawn.

Later that night, the electricity finally went out. Thomas and Lucy had taken the watch. Janine, Christian, and Henry sat in the lounge, sharing a bottle of wine and more of Thomas' weed. Everyone else had gone to bed.

"Shit! It's pitch black in here!" said Henry. He tripped over a coffee table and a glass smashed on the floor.

"Quiet!" shouted Janine.

A lone emergency light that still had a bit of battery juice kicked on in the back corner of the giant room, behind a partition. It provided just enough light for their eyes to adjust.

"There are candles in the kitchen, why don't you go find them, Henry, since you're so good with drawers. Christian, would you go check with Lucy, I'll go to the south entrance and talk to Thomas," Janine said authoritatively.

"Whoa who put you in cha…"

"Dude, just shut up and get the candles." Christian lost his usual easygoing demeanor.

Janine made her way to the south entrance. Thomas was standing inside the doorway. "Shh, there's a ship going over," he whispered.

"The electricity went out."

"I know, the streetlights all went out, too. They must have finally realized leaving the grid intact was only helping us." Thomas crept to the door and peeked upward. "It's passed. It was headed north over the building. I hope Lucy is inside."

"What should we do? Should we wake everyone up and get ready to fight?"

Thomas stood in the doorway. He turned toward Janine. "I'm not too worried, they're just patrolli…" Blood gushed out of Thomas' mouth. He looked down at the bloody, gore-covered fingers sticking out of his chest. They slowly began to withdraw back inside of him. He looked up at Janine, his mouth open, a stunned look in his eyes. He collapsed.

Janine didn't stop to see the bug that had just killed Thomas. She turned and ran as fast as she could. *I've got to get Emily. She can't go back there.* The kitchen was closer. She ran in, startling Henry and Christian lighting a candle. "They're here!" Janine ran out the other end of the kitchen toward the bunk area.

"Molly!" Christian yelled and ran after Janine.

As they neared the bunks, they heard Henry scream. Janine ran to Emily's bunk and shook her awake. "The bugs are here!" She grabbed her pack and a rifle from her own bunk.

Emily was still in bed.

"Come on!" Janine grabbed Emily's arm and yanked her to her feet. "Shoes, now!"

Something grabbed Janine from behind. The bug ripped the pack and rifle out of her hands and flung them across the room. It stuffed Janine in a huge sack it carried on its back. Moments later Emily was shoved in.

"Fuck!" Janine flung herself upward, clawing toward the opening of the sack.

"Ow! Stop, you're hurting me!" Emily yelled.

They felt the bug moving. Lucy, Molly, and Pixie were shoved into the sack. Molly's elbow hit Janine on the nose, and it started bleeding.

"Oh my gahd oh my gahd what the fuck…" Pixie screamed.

Janine maneuvered her arm so she could clutch her nose. The blood seeped onto Lucy's back. They jostled each other for air, Janine bled, Pixie screamed.

"I can't breathe," someone gasped.

Ten agonizing minutes later, they were turned upside down and dumped unceremoniously onto a hard metal surface. Janine saw dawn breaking through the slatted walls of the transport ship. She hugged Emily, who huddled in a fetal position and moaned. Molly yelled at Pixie to stop screaming. Lucy cradled Janine and Emily.

"They're going to… Ohh gahd…" Emily groaned. The ship lifted off the ground. Emily leaned back and looked at the sky. "It's so beautiful… We're never going to see it again…"

The ship came down on the roof of a building that looked from the outside like the slaughterhouses they had bombed the night before.

The side of the ship opened, and two bugs walked on. They carried long, slender poles, with three prongs at the end. As they walked toward the women, one of the bugs pressed a button and white-hot electricity sizzled between the prongs. It aimed the prod at the three huddled on the floor together. They didn't move fast enough. Lucy screamed as the prongs bit into her flesh. The bug pulled the prod away and a wisp of smoke rose from her shoulder. She jumped up and started to run toward the back of the ship, but the bug grabbed her and shoved her forward. It aimed the prod at Janine and Emily. They got up and walked slowly, holding each other. The bug didn't think they were going fast enough and prodded Emily in the lower back. She screamed and jerked forward. Janine followed.

They were herded off the ship, where one by one, a third bug picked them up and ripped off their clothes, then shoved them toward a fourth bug who tagged their ears, then pushed them toward an opening in the fence that led to a ramp down the side of the building. Emily screamed for Janine as the bug pulled them apart and stripped her. The bug finished tearing off Emily's clothes and pushed her along, then grabbed Janine. The bug stuck a finger down the neck of her shirt and ripped down the front, then pulled it off her like a jacket. Janine felt a sharp burning where the fabric had pulled against the back of her neck. She screamed when the bug began pulling at her jeans. It pulled and tore through the button and zipper, then grabbed a pant leg each with two arms and tugged them off in one motion. Once Janine was naked, it shoved her toward the fourth bug. It grabbed her by the head and torso. The image of Kalinda getting her head ripped off flashed through Janine's mind. The bug stuck a small contraption up to her ear. Janine felt a sharp pain. She reached up and felt a large plastic tag attached to her ear. It was round and had a series of bumps. The bug shoved her toward the ramp. She caught up with Emily and they grasped each other again. Yet another bug herded them down.

At the bottom of the ramp, two bugs grabbed Janine and Emily and pulled them apart again. The bug that had Janine had a machine that looked like a thick tennis racket. It held the scanner up to her lower abdomen. After a few moments, the bug made a slight clicking sound and put the scanner aside, and picked up a probe. It held Janine with three arms, pulling apart her legs. It inserted the probe roughly inside her. Janine screamed. After a moment it made more clicking sounds to itself, and removed the probe. Moments later another bug came over, carrying what looked like a metal baster. Janine screamed again. The first bug pushed her down onto what looked like a modern-art version of a gynecologist's table. It strapped her down and pulled her legs apart again, strapping them to two arms that extended from the end of the table.

Emily screamed, "Janine!" and struggled against

the bug that was holding her and scanning her.

Janine started sobbing. The bug inserted a hard, rough finger into her anus. She felt blood well up as the creature felt around for her uterus. It inserted the baster into her vagina and Janine felt cool liquid spurt inside her. The bug unstrapped her and roughly pushed her to the second bug, who dragged her by a leg to a cart and tossed her in.

Janine landed in the cart and collapsed, her arms out in front of her, head resting on one arm. She sobbed quietly, her body heaving. After a few excruciatingly long minutes, the bug deposited her into a small pen with several other women. There were troughs of water and a mushy yellow grain. Janine immediately noticed an awful stench. The women shared a bucket for a toilet. There was nothing to wipe with. She curled up in a corner and cried herself to sleep.

The next day, a bug scanned Janine with the racket-looking device again. It strapped her to the rape rack again and repeated the process from the morning before. It did it again on the third day. Finally, on the fourth day, after Janine was scanned, the bug instead took her down a floor, and put her into another pen with six other women. There were the same troughs and bucket as the first pen. Two women stood eating at the grain trough. Janine saw another woman sitting apart, who had shit crusted on her ass and the backs of her thighs, like she had sat in her own diarrhea and it had dried on her.

A chubby woman with dark-brown, wavy hair picked up a handful of yellow mush from the trough and walked over. She offered the handful to Janine. "I'm Beth. You're probably hungry. It's not bad once you get used to it. Kinda like plain rice."

Janine hesitantly took the handful of mush. "Th-thank you. I'm Janine. I… I've had it already."

"Oh, of course, don't mind me. I just see a new girl and I feel like I have to help her get used to things."

"It's, it's okay, I didn't mean…"

"No, I know what you meant. It's alright. Let me introduce you to the girls. Over at the trough are Mary and Sarah. Sarah is only eleven, go easy on her." said Beth.

Janine looked more closely. She hadn't noticed one of the women was actually a young girl. "Eleven?" she exclaimed.

"Yep, poor thing just got her period this year. That didn't stop the aliens from sticking her on the rape rack like the rest of us. If you're fertile, they'll want to milk you," Beth explained.

"That's terrible," said Janine.

"Well all of this is terrible. Anyway, the girl with explosive diarrhea is Linda, stay far away from her for now, we don't know if it's catching. Over here are Anna and Dolores."

A short, stout woman with pendulous breasts

and thick, almost black, curly hair waved at Janine. "I'm Dolores. You look very new to all of this."

"Yes. I was captured… I don't even know how many days ago anymore."

"You were just captured? How did you not get caught until now?" said Anna, a stick-thin, blond, straight-haired version of Dolores.

"I… We…" Janine stuttered. "I'm sorry, this is just, so awful…"

"I know, hon. I know." Dolores patted Janine on the shoulder. "We've got to make the best of this…"

Mary, the older of the two at the trough, turned with an angry look on her face. "Make the best of it? They're fucking *farming* us like fucking cows! How the hell do we make the best of this? Should I make some tea and cookies?" She threw the handful of yellow mush she had been eating on the floor. "Make the best of *that*!"

"I'm sorry, honey, I'm just trying to…"

"*Make the best of things?* Yeah, right. You can't make the best of this. There is no best to this. The best thing that could have happened to me is if they had just killed me outright. I'd rather be dead than live like this!" Mary shouted.

Sarah, the eleven-year-old, started crying and collapsed to the floor.

"Oh my poor thing!" Dolores ambled over to her and embraced her, rocking her back and forth.

Sarah clutched at Dolores. "I want to die!"

"Oh honey…" Dolores just rocked Sarah until she stopped sobbing.

Janine ran a hand through her hair and sighed. She dejectedly walked to a corner, curled into a ball, and fell asleep.

~

After a few months, a bug started coming every day to check if the women were lactating yet. The bug would grab a woman, and painfully squeeze a breast to see if anything leaked. Janine started leaking colostrum in the seventh month of her pregnancy. That day, when the bug came to check, she was brought down another floor. The bug roughly attached a shackle to her leg, then picked up two hoses with suction cups at the ends. The hoses were attached to a machine, which the bug switched on. A sucking noise came from the hoses. It stuck the suction cups to Janine's breasts and she cried out in pain. The powerful suction was relentless. She watched as a thin stream of thick, yellowish liquid ran down the hoses to the machine. Once she was sucked dry, the pain got worse. She tried to pull them off, but the suction held them on. The bug didn't come back and turn off the machine for another half an hour. When it took the suction cups off her breasts, they were purple.

Every day, three times a day, this process was

repeated. After a week or so, Janine started producing regular white milk. Her breasts were so painfully engorged that she came to welcome the milkings. When she was unshackled and brought back to the pen she shared with fourteen other women, and girls, she would curl up in a corner and try to sleep. Most of the time she ended up staring at the wall for hours.

Then the day came when she started having contractions. The milkings had been done for the day and Janine was sitting against a wall, when she was wracked by a tidal wave of pain in her gut. When she winced and cried out, another woman looked up.

"You gonna pop?"

"I think so."

The woman stood up slowly, clutching her back and her own very pregnant belly. She waddled over to Janine. "I'm Stacey. I'm sorry I haven't introduced myself before. This place kind of sucks the life out of you." Her face twisted. "That's an understatement I guess. Here, lean back against the wall and try to breathe."

Janine felt a rush of wetness between her legs.

"Oh your water broke already! This baby is coming!" Stacey gathered straw into a pile. "Lay down here."

Janine cried out as the contractions grew to less than ten seconds apart. She tried to breathe deeply, and vomited on herself. She didn't even try to wipe it off. She screamed, steeled herself, and pushed. She felt herself rip open as the baby's head slid out. She screamed again, then pushed as hard as she could. Stacey caught the baby as it came out.

"It's a girl. Poor thing, she's going to just end up being bred like us." Stacey placed her in Janine's arms.

Janine looked down at this tiny person. She immediately fell in love. She poked the tiny hand with a finger, and the baby closed her own fist around it.

"Kalinda. Her name is Kalinda." Janine sighed.

"That's a beautiful name." Stacey wiped a gob of blood and vomit from the back of the baby's head.

"She's not going to grow up to this. We're going to get out of here and bring these fuckers down."

Janine lifted the baby to her breast, and began to feed her. She smiled and stroked the tiny head.

She woke up the next morning to little Kalinda quietly crying in her arms. She cuddled and soothed her, holding her close for warmth.

When a bug came to take the baby and the placenta away, Janine did her best not to let go, but it was futile. The bug smacked her in the face twice with one hand as it pried her arms open and pulled Kalinda away with a fourth. Janine cried out and chased the bug to the door of the pen, which it slammed in her face. She collapsed, sobbing. Stacey and one of the other girls came over and tried to comfort her.

Later that morning, at the first milking time, the bug had to literally drag her to the rows of milking machines. After that, they moved her to a pen on the other side of the milking floor with other women who had given birth but were still producing milk.

Janine could barely eat for weeks. She lost weight and after two months her milk production waned. That was when they brought her back up to the insemination floor and started force feeding her.

~

When she gave birth a second time, Janine didn't name the boy. One of the women in the pen suggested she call him "Veal". Janine put the baby down and tried to get up and attack her, but two other women held her down until she calmed down.

When the bug came, she didn't fight. She just cried.

After three more years, and three more pregnancies, Janine's body began to give out. When she was at twenty-four weeks of her last pregnancy, she went into premature labor. She couldn't sit up to hold the baby, so the other women placed it on her chest. She weakly embraced the tiny premature baby, then felt a rush of warm fluid come out of her.

"Oh shit she's bleeding!"

Janine heard other women exclaim and one screamed. As she lay on the floor, she began to feel very distant. The voices around her began to fade.

Janine's last thought as she lost consciousness

was, *So this must be how the cows feel in their last moments…*

Part Three

Captain Sebon paced on four legs, back and forth in her lounge with a cup of capulus in hand. Only five local years on this planet and the atmosphere was already starting to collapse. Sebon didn't like handing out layoff slips. She mind-probed Vayo, the shift supervisor on duty. *I need to see you in my lounge as soon as possible.*

Vayo's reply came almost immediately. *Yes ma'am!*

Ugh, Vayo is such a suck up, I'm glad I don't have to work with his sycophant ass much longer, thought Sebon. She walked to the table and popped a piece of stultus from her breakfast tray into her mouth.

I'm here! Vayo's mind probe was nauseatingly excited.

Come in.

Vayo opened the door as she thought *in.*

Sebon ate more of her breakfast as she thought, *Vayo, the planet's atmosphere is collapsing already. It's time to pack up and let the mining companies take over. I've got layoff slips for you to hand out.*

Vayo's six shoulders slumped. *Yes ma'am.*

Sebon continued, *Coordinate with the local dairy farms to transfer their stock and workers to our slaughterhouses. We'll need to be running the plants at full capacity around the clock. I'll want your recommendations for workers to whom you think we should offer the night shift supervisory positions. Remind them supervisory jobs are a permanent position with AgriCorp. No more bidding for contracts.*

Vayo sent an affirmative mind probe, then paused before thinking, *So, uhhh, ma'am, about that promotion I put in for, did you…*

Yes, yes, I gave them my recommendation on the subject. The higher ups said there's just nothing that fits you at this time, Sebon thought irritatedly.

Vayo persisted, *Ma'am, they've been saying that every year for…*

I know. There's nothing more I can do for you, Vayo. That will be all for now.

Vayo almost replied, then decided against it. He dejectedly turned and left the captain's lounge.

Sebon finished her breakfast and poured another cup of capulus. She reflected on her five years on Farm Planet A3427H. Just a few months after arriving, Captains Terb and Ligus had gone missing, and Sebon had been promoted to Captain. Just a couple of weeks after that, feral stultus had bombed three slaughterhouses. It hadn't caused too much damage, and they had captured the stultus that same night. The slaughterhouses were down for just a week, during which time six others in nearby regions were simply kept open for three shifts to handle the overflow.

Sebon had opened six more feedlots and an equal number of breeding facilities. Her breeding program had been a complete success. This species of stultus was most succulent at three years of age, so for two years she had been producing a steady, growing supply of meat.

Unfortunately, the stultus on this planet didn't reach breeding age for about ten years, so she wouldn't be able to take pride in the dairy stock she had produced for captains to the north and east, before the planet was uninhabitable, and the stultus would all be slaughtered. That was alright, though, she had made a good name for herself here, and hopefully it would be reflected in the end-of-contract bonus. She figured she'd spring for a spa planet this coming vacation. She could use some spoiling.

Sebon finished her cup of capulus and stretched, preparing for a day of inspecting slaughterhouses, feedlots, and breeding facilities. Oh, there was that meeting with the Eastern dairy Captain this morning, too. It was going to be a busy day.

~

The Quaestui worker pushed the cart of stultus babies down the aisle. There had been six already today. *Damn stultus bitches were busy last night. If I have to empty the shit buckets one more time this week...*

She pulled open the door to a pen. *Shit, another*

one. Oh, this one's a runt. Hammer time! She tossed the runt in with the six other babies, to be disposed of later. *Oh, looks like we got a downer in here.* She picked up the stultus's limp body. *Shit, it's dead!*

She pulled the body out of the pen, smacked back a pregnant stultus who tried to run out the door, and dropped the body on the floor in the aisle to be picked up by the dead cart later. She moved on to the next pen and checked for babies.

There's a lot of blood to clean up. I suppose I'll get stuck taking care of that, too, she thought as she moved down the aisle.

~

One month later, every remaining stultus and pecus on the planet had been slaughtered and packed into refrigeration ships. Mining companies began to arrive. Desalination ships began filtering the oceans into huge tankers. Buildings were broken down for materials and packed onto freighters. Workers filed onto their ships, ate one last meal, then most of them brushed their teeth. Stasis capsules sighed closed. Captains set coordinates and began liftoff sequences.

In what was left of a small town next to a large river near the east coast of a continent in the northern hemisphere, a ship pulled out of the ground for the first time in five years. Dirt and debris rained down as the massive silver bulk rose into the sky.

Once in orbit, Captain Sebon double checked that everything was as it should be, and lay down in her stasis capsule. Her last thought as she drifted off was of a woman, on a beach...

and other tales…

Blame It On The Drugs

My name's Billy. I'm an addict. I'd tell you my sob story, but you've probably heard it a million times before. Good kid, good grades, one mistake at a party, blah blah blah, life ruined. I'm not looking for any sympathy. I own my mistakes.

My grandma's a sweet lady. She raised me. My mom died when I was born. My dad blamed me for her death and skipped town. Grandma understands I need my medicine, so she helps me out. She's on Social Security, but her place is rent controlled, so that saves her enough to keep me from getting the shakes. She didn't mind me staying with her after I turned eighteen, but the landlord is a dick and said he'd kick her out if I didn't go. She was ready to find a new place, but I said that was okay, I'd find a place to stay. I stay with my friend Manny now. We go to a shooting gallery on Clark Street, an old, abandoned church. Our dealer, Sam, squats there. There's usually fifteen to twenty folks crashing with him at any given time. Sammy the Surgeon, we call him. He was a medic in the army. Now he's our medic.

Anyway, word got around this morning that Sam had some exotic new horse he wanted everyone to try, so he was letting it go for dirt cheap. I swung by

Grandma's and got twenty bucks off her, and we headed to Clark Street. It was busy. There must have been fifty people altogether, smoking butts on the church steps, waiting in line along the left wall to see Sammy in the back office, cooking, sprawled in a pew with a needle in their arm, there were even a couple of folks in the confessional booth, moaning and rocking the thing back and forth.

Manny and I got in line. I looked over the pews, and thought I saw the back of my friend Heidi's head. "Heidi!" I called. When she turned to me, I saw that she was gnawing frantically on her fingernails.

"Oh, hi Billy, Manny." She took her fingers out of her mouth long enough to greet us. The tips of her index and middle fingers were a little bloody. "How you guys doin'?" Her fingers went back into her mouth and she turned away.

Okay, that was Heidi for you, I guess. She always was a bit of a nervous wreck.

Manny and I got to the front of the line when bloodcurdling screams exploded from the confessional booth. A few people jerked their heads in that direction, but no one did anything. I wanted to see if I could help, but we were at the front of the line. A minute later the screams subsided and were replaced by moans of ecstasy.

Geoff, Sammy's goon, was standing outside the office door. He shot us a look. "Okay, you boys are up." He held the office door open for us.

We filed in. Sammy sat behind a massive oak desk, obviously left by whatever priest ran this place when it was a functioning church. His receding hairline didn't stop him from pulling his long, dark-brown hair back into a ponytail. He pushed his glasses up his nose and looked up at us. "Good morning, gentlemen. As I'm sure you've heard, I'm running a special. Brand new stuff. Three bucks a pop. What do you say, boys?"

I handed him my twenty, and Manny dropped a ten on the desk. Sammy opened a drawer, counted out ten tiny packets, and handed them to me. I stuck them in my pocket, said thanks, and we high tailed it out of there. Sometimes we stay and cook at the church, but it was too crowded today, and my nerves weren't in the mood for it.

When we opened the first packet, we found the junk was a deep red. I'd never seen down that color before. I shrugged and dumped it in the spoon. When I mixed it with water and cooked it, it looked like blood. Manny and I agreed it was just the nature of the new, exotic stuff Sammy had gotten. We shared a needle full. I lay back on my mattress and felt like I was sinking into the bed. Manny moaned that this was pretty good stuff but he didn't understand the hype…

~

I woke up craving pork chops. Manny said he could go for some too, so we headed to Grandma's. She happened to have a six pack on hand. We were so hungry we asked her to cook all six for us. Grandma is such a sweet lady, she agreed no problem.

As Manny and I chowed down on pork chops, it occurred to me that this wasn't even really satisfying my craving. I asked Grandma what else she had. She said she had leg of lamb, plenty of steak, and a full rack of pork ribs in the downstairs freezer. It didn't take much convincing to talk her into cooking up the ribs for us, after all, my grandma, she's a bit of a pushover, to be honest… yeah, I probably take advantage sometimes.

By the time Manny and I got home from dinner at Grandma's, we were ready for another hit. We shot up and fell asleep with full stomachs and something nagging at us.

~

When I woke up, I realized I'd been nibbling on my fingers in my sleep. Oh man, that tasted divine. I was stunned. I didn't know what to think. Was I really craving human flesh? They say humans taste a lot like pigs. That would explain the massive pork cravings. *Nah,* I thought, *it must just be the taste of blood. I need more meat.*

Manny woke up and I asked him what he

thought. His fingertips were bloody, too.

"Do you think… Ah shit, man, are we craving blood?" I asked.

"Man, I don't know! Just that my fingers tasted really fucking good this morning."

"Yeah, me too. Shit, this is fucked up."

"Let's cook, and worry about it later."

Manny cooked up a batch for the two of us, and we decided to head over to Grandma's to see if some nice, bloody steak wouldn't take care of our hunger. Grandma didn't really want to cook them too rare, but I explained that we were really craving it bloody, so she finally agreed. She thawed the steaks and I was tempted to try mine raw, to be honest. I'm not that crazy, though, so she seared them in a pan for us and we sat down to eat.

"This is good, but I'm still not feeling satisfied, man," said Manny as he chewed.

He was right, as bloody as the steaks were, they just weren't doing it for me, either.

~

That afternoon, we were running low on junk, so we took a trip to see Sammy. The church wasn't too busy. A few regulars were hanging out in the pews, including Heidi.

"Hey Heidi!" I called.

She turned to look and brightened up at the sight

of us. "Manny! Billy! How ya doin'?" she said as she picked up a pair of crutches from the floor. As she stood to come chat with us, we saw that her leg was gone, from just above the knee.

"What happened, woman? You get in an accident?" I exclaimed.

"Nah, Billy, I just got really hungry. Sammy helped me out. He was a medic, you know?" Heidi lifted her fingers to her mouth and chewed nervously.

"Haha, okay, that's a good one. Really, what happened?"

Heidi took her fingers out of her mouth and looked at me funny. "It's not a joke… Say, you guys wanna come get high with me later? I got some of that great stuff, knocks you right out…"

"Nah, thanks, though." I gave Manny a look. "We gotta go catch Sammy. Talk to you later, girl."

"Yeah guys, great seein' ya…" As she turned away, she started gnawing on her fingers again.

Geoff was in his usual spot. "Hey Billy, Manny." He opened the door for us and we walked in.

"Hello boys, I don't suppose you're in need of medical services?" Sammy grinned, revealing a pair of gold crowns where his incisors used to be.

"Naw, man, just the usual." I dropped $60 on the desk.

"Well, well, well, big spenders today," Sammy said as he counted out twenty tiny packets. "Do let me know if you need any other services in the near future, boys."

"Okay, sure man, thanks." Manny and I hightailed it out of there. We walked home as quickly as we could.

"What is going on today, man? First Heidi is missing a leg all of a sudden, then Sammy's trying to talk us into some medical shit? Man, I need to get high ASAP." Manny fumbled as he opened a packet. "It's more of that red stuff."

After Manny cooked and we shot up, I laid on the couch thinking. I didn't realize I was chewing on my fingers again until I moaned with pleasure at the taste. I sat up suddenly. "What if we're craving human flesh, dude?"

"What? That's insane, man." Manny absentmindedly chewed on his middle finger.

"Look at what you're doing!" I yelled at him.

Manny took his finger out of his mouth and gaped at the bloody fingertip. "Oh my gahd, man, no way. No way."

"What are we gonna do, we can't just eat people!" I exclaimed.

"Heidi… Heidi ate her own leg, dude! That's what she was talking about!"

"Oh my gahd!"

"Holy shit!"

"Fuck, man, what the hell's going on? Is it the…" My face fell. "Sammy asked if we needed any medical services. He was offering to cut our legs off for us!"

"No way, man, that's crazy!"

"There's no way I'm eating human flesh, even my own, that's too crazy. I need another hit, man."

Manny cooked again and we shared another needle full of the blood-red heroin.

"Dude, do you think it could be the junk, that's making us want..."

"Shit. You're right. We can't use any more of this shit!" Manny picked up the remaining packets and threw them in the trash.

~

A few hours later Manny and I were digging through the trash.

"That's all eighteen packets. Phew!"

"What were we thinking, tossing out perfectly good dope?"

"Yeah, I can't ask Grandma for more money 'til we use this up anyway. Sammy practically gives it away for that price, too, man."

"Yeah, so, what about these cravings?"

"For people? I don't know man, it's pretty intense, but we can ignore it, right? Willpower and shit."

"Yeah, willpower."

~

A couple days later we were down to flipping a coin to see who would get his leg cut off. We went to Grandma's and got some more money and took off to Clark Street.

Sammy doled out our dope then peered up at us expectantly.

Manny and I looked at each other and sighed. "We decided to flip a coin," I said dejectedly.

"I see, well, gentlemen, I'll flip. Who's calling?"

I looked at Manny. "You call, dude."

"Heads."

Sammy picked up a quarter from his desk and tossed it in the air. He caught it deftly and slapped it onto the top of his other hand. "Are you sure about this, boys?"

Manny and I exchanged looks again. "Yeah." Manny sighed.

Sammy lifted his hand. The coin had landed heads up. Manny groaned.

"It's okay, I've got anesthetic, and plenty of bandages for you to take with you so you can keep it clean. I've even got crutches for you. There were a cache of them, and wheelchairs in the basement of the church, it turns out. They collected them for charity or something."

Manny groaned again. "Okay man, let's get this over with."

~

I carried the bag with Manny's leg in it as we made our way to Grandma's. "She'll understand. She'll cook this up for us real nice."

"Don't you think we should ration it? I don't want to cut off my other leg any time soon."

"Yeah, good point, man."

When we got to Grandma's I explained what was going on. Grandma's such a sweet lady, she said she understood, that we needed to do what we needed to do to get by. I gave her Manny's leg and she said she'd clean it up good for us. We went into her living room and shot up while she got started. I turned on the TV. There was some report about a guy killing his neighbor and eating him.

"What is wrong with some people? My gahd!" Manny said as we watched the police pushing the man out of his house in handcuffs. "I could never kill someone, no matter how bad the craving got, man."

"I know, right? That shit's just too far dude, too far," I agreed.

~

A week later, we ran out of Manny meat. The cravings didn't go away, they got worse.

"What are we gonna do now?" I opined.

"Well for starters you could cut your leg off this time," Manny suggested.

I didn't really like the idea. I saw how Manny struggled to get around with his crutches all the time. "Sammy said they have wheelchairs at the church, we should get you one," I said.

"What? No way! We are not cutting off my other leg before you give up one of yours, man!"

"No, dude, relax, I was just thinking it would be easier for you to get around," I lied. "You know, Grandma is such a sweet lady, I bet she'd be willing to help us out here."

"You really think so?" asked Manny.

"I do think so. Let's go pay her a visit."

We walked to Grandma's and I explained my idea. She was a little hesitant at first, but then she said she just loves me so much, she'd do anything for me. That's my Grandma. I got her her coat and the three of us headed to Clark Street.

Sammy was very gracious to Grandma. He gave her extra anesthetic, and while she was recovering, he had Geoff haul some crutches and a wheelchair up from the basement. When Grandma woke up, she was beside herself, and wouldn't stop thanking Sammy for his generosity. She's such a sweet lady. I pushed her home in her new wheelchair. When we got there, she insisted on cooking her leg for us. I told her she should rest, let me do it, but she insisted!

Manny and I ate like kings for another week. Grandma came up with some great recipes. We had BBQ Grandma sandwiches one night, Grandma steaks with potatoes and carrots another night. She even made us spaghetti bolognese with her leg meat! Grandma's such a great cook. I love her so much.

~

After we ran out of Grandma's leg, we figured we'd try and go without for a while. Sammy sold out of the red stuff, so we figured it would wear off.

The next time we went to the church, Heidi was outside in a wheelchair. Both of her legs were gone. She chewed frantically at her fingers. "Hi guys!"

Manny and I just exchanged a look and went inside. There weren't too many people around. The few that were there were missing legs or arms, one fat guy even had a huge bandage around his midsection, like he'd had some of his gut removed. I'll bet that fatty, crispy, bacony flesh was divine…

We went in to see Sammy. All he had was $5 bags. That was fine. We gave him fifty bucks and he counted out ten for us.

It was quiet at the church so we decided to cook there for a change. After we shot up, we laid around on the pews for a while. Heidi came in and wheeled herself over to Geoff. Geoff shook his head no at her. They argued for a while, but Geoff just kept shaking his head no.

"Please! Just one arm! I only need one!" Heidi screeched.

Geoff shook his head no again. Heidi started sobbing as she wheeled herself away.

"Damn, poor girl is desperate," Manny commented.

"Yeah, I hope we don't get like that. I am kind of hungry, though..."

~

Manny and I tried to go without. After the third day, I woke up and I'd gnawed half of my left index finger off. We went to Grandma's and explained what was going on. Grandma's so wonderful she said to take her other leg. We wheeled her to Clark Street and Sammy took care of us.

~

After another week we ran out of Grandma meat again. Manny suggested luring a homeless guy to our place. I was really hesitant. That's murder after all. After a few hours of thinking about it, though, I was so hungry, I said let's do it. We went down by the river and talked a drunk into coming over to "party". When he was sitting in the armchair I came up behind him and smashed him on the head with a baseball bat. It didn't kill him, just knocked him out. Manny and I laid out a tarp, and dragged the homeless man onto it.

"How should we kill him?" Manny asked.

"Well, how about I hold him down and you hold a pillow over his face?" I suggested.

"Alright."

I retrieved a pillow and handed it to Manny, then sat down on the guy's torso, pinning his arms to the floor. Manny got down on knee and stump and placed the pillow over the guy's face. He pressed down and the guy began to struggle. I held him down best I could until he stopped struggling. Manny held the pillow on his face for a few more minutes, just to be sure.

Now came the messy part. We couldn't exactly carry a whole body to Grandma's without being seen. Manny had a hacksaw. We stripped the guy's clothes off and cut his limbs off. When he was just a head and torso, we cut that in half and tossed the guts in the garbage. We stuffed all the parts in garbage bags and stuffed those in duffel bags. It was a good thing Grandma had a big freezer, that was for sure.

~

The homeless guy fed us well for a couple of months. Manny and I felt bad, but we had to eat, right? We also had to shoot up. When we got to the shooting gallery, half a dozen folks were outside smoking butts. Every one of them was missing a limb or two. We got inside, and Heidi was there in her wheelchair.

A guy was shooting her up in her one remaining arm.

We hightailed it past her, and saw some guys playing Russian roulette. I guess the loser gets eaten…

Sammy greeted us kindly. "Good afternoon, gentlemen. How's Grandma?" A gunshot rang out back in the church proper.

I dropped $50 on the desk. "Grandma's good. She's such a sweet lady."

"She sure is. Bring her around some time for a visit!" Sammy counted out our dope.

On the way out, the confessional was rocking again, moans coming from within. As we passed it, the door crashed open and a couple of naked double amputees fell out. We kept walking.

Excerpts From Cinch's Diary

May 19th, I think.

They call me Cinch. I'm just one of the guys. I like to pay attention to what goes on in this town. There are some pretty bad people around, and some that pass through. They like to beat people down for how they were born. That type. I see a lot. It makes me so angry but I can't do a lot about it.

Most of the time I'm at the bar with my friends. My friends are good people. They understand that my ADHD makes me hard to handle at times. Sometimes I won't stop talking, but my conversations go everywhere, like, tangents. My one friend Annie, she's a bartender at my favorite place, O'Grady's. She takes good care of me. She'd give you the shirt off her back, so sometimes we actually trade shirts. I guess I'd give the shirt off my back, too. Hahaha. Annie gets harassed sometimes when she's closing up the bar, so sometimes I stay with her and walk her home. So does my buddy Bird. He's a weird one, but he's a writer, and they say writers are weird. Hey I guess since my therapist told me to do this diary, I'm a writer, too! Haha! Anyway, Annie's real pretty but she'd never be my girlfriend. That's okay, I like being alone. I've never had luck with women for long. I have this one ex…

Shit, I was talking about the bad people. Maybe I should go down to the bar, see if I can score some Adderall. I'll write more later.

May 20th, 2019, 5:06 a.m.
The filth will know me and they will fear me. This scum-ridden town will whisper my name in back alleys and dive bars… They will call me… I need a better name. I can't use my daytime nickname. I don't even know if I should be writing this, I don't want Cinch to read this. Ah hell, Cinch can't concentrate long enough to read anything.

Tonight was a little busier than usual. After I was able to get an Adderall through Annie, I came home and, having been able to remember the passcode, went to the basement. There I shed my daytime skin and got into uniform. I took my hammer, Josie, out, and went to the rooftops. I crouched in my usual place next to the neon hotel sign, and I didn't have very much time for reflection before the first pond scum showed itself. A crackhead accosted a woman outside the hotel, and followed her down the street. I silently shimmied down the fire escape and unzipped my purse. When I rounded the corner, the crackhead had the woman by the arm, and was dragging her towards the alley. I hitched up my dress and ran toward them. The crackhead pulled the woman into the alley just as I reached them. It was the perfect cover. I gave the crackhead a swift right with Josie, and he went down. The woman screamed and ran. Good. It gave me enough time to strip the crackhead naked, bind him up by his hands and feet over a trash can, and shove a fat, red, silicone buttplug right up his ass, before the cops showed up.

I returned to the rooftops and decided to prowl for a while. The night did not disappoint. I made it three blocks, winding my way between chimneys and stairwells, pigeon cages and laundry lines. I leapt effortlessly over the streets below, my dress billowing out as I practically floated between roofs. After the post office, I spied a group of neo-nazi scum out for some trouble. I climbed hand by hand silently down a drainage pipe, and followed them, slipping between doorways and alleys, remaining unseen and unheard.

They did not disappoint. A Black man came stumbling drunkenly out of a bar, and the fascist pieces of shit started harassing him. It didn't take long for one of them to throw a punch. The man went down and I hiked up my skirts and pulled out Josie. I plunged into the middle of the group of five skinhead scum and spun 360 degrees, whacking four out of five, with the last one jumping out of the way at the last second. One of them hunched over, holding his cracked skull. Another howled in pain as his left arm hung limp. The remaining three regrouped and came back at me.

I swung Josie in an underhand arc, right into the first neo-nazi's balls. He let out a loud croak and went down. The next two leapt at me from either side. Josie came up and smashed the one to the right in the chin, as the one to the left landed a punch on the left side of my face. I didn't even look as I grabbed his fist with my left hand and crushed it. He squealed like a mouse caught in a cat's jaws, and swung at me with his other hand. I smacked that hand away and landed Josie square on his nose. Meanwhile, the other two scum had regrouped. The one with the bad arm kicked me in the balls. I went down, and started laughing. He kicked me again and again as I rolled around laughing hysterically. Cracked-skull guy joined in and I grabbed his foot and pushed him off balance. I swung around and brought Josie down on bad-arm guy's foot. I jumped back up and smacked cracked-skull guy across the head again with Josie. It was over. Three were out like lights, and two were writhing in pain on the ground. I disrobed all of them, then pulled rope out of my purse.

When the cops found them, they were lying in a circle, all unconscious, with a hand between the guy in front's legs, cupping his balls. It would have made a pretty picture. I would have called it "Synchronized Ball Cupping, a Statement on Toxic Masculinity and White Supremacy."

I suppose I should put out the fire and go home

now, I think my dress is dry. I like to wash it in the river. It helps wash away the negative energy from all the filth in this town. Until next time…
-The Pursed Avenger, for now

Friday, maybe. I'm hung over.
Me when I'm on Adderall doesn't think I know about me when I'm on Adderall. I guess 'cause I'm a lot smarter and stronger then, I kind of look down on myself now. Hell, I look down on myself right now. I take meds for that, too, and the schizophrenia. Only Adderall gives me the super strength. I like it when I feel like that. Annie said when I'm like that I am a superhero, like in the movies! She's the only one who knows. Not even my therapist knows. I'm glad I don't never have to show this to my therapist. He'd think I was crazy. Haha. My ex never knew because I wasn't on Adderall back then. She used to hit me a lot. I never hit her back though, because I don't hit women. Well I guess unless I was on Adderall and there was a very bad woman I would have to hit her…

May 25th, 2019, 4:36 a.m.
Tonight after I took the Adderall, I perched on the roof of the local pharmacy. Sometimes junkies like to try and break in. Tonight I caught one such character, and left him bound on the steps of a church that has NA meetings and a good reputation for getting people to go to rehab. Junkies don't

deserve compromising positions, or even always arrest. They've got a disease, and are self-medicating, akin to why I drink when I'm Cinch. They don't deserve to be mistreated by the police.

After taking care of the junkie, I made my way to the roof of O'Grady's. Annie wasn't working tonight. I like to keep an eye on the place for her.

Before too long, a group of eight rednecks pulled up in four of their dick replacements. Blazing roof lights, jacked up frames, and loud exhausts, these trucks are a beacon for small penis syndrome. I knew I would get to have some real fun tonight. These guys are almost always itching for a fight to prove their manliness to one another.

I snuck down the back fire escape and settled myself into the bushes to the side of O'Grady's, where I could remain unseen but still hear everything going down inside through an open window. It wasn't too long before I heard one of the dickless boys start harassing a local translady, Cynthia. She asked him to leave her alone, but the guy kept insisting he wanted to know if she was "still a man down there" so he could punch her. When I heard cloth rip I sprinted around the corner and into O'Grady's. I grabbed the one pissant by the neck and slammed his head against the bar. That was a mistake. Skeeto was working. He shrieked and hit me over the head with a bottle of whiskey. I don't blame Skeeto. He gets his name because his voice and personality are as whiny as one of those little, flying, blood-sucking assholes. It took me only a moment to recover, but in that moment seven other redneck pieces of shit were on me. I pulled out Josie just as one of them hit me across the back with a chair. Josie went flying across the room. I stood up straight and flung a fist 180 degrees into the guy's face. He went down, but I still had six more to contend with. I leapt for Josie but one of the pieces of shit grabbed my dress and I fell to the ground. I felt a boot come down on my head, and several kicks in my ribs. My jaw hit the floor with a crack and I spit out a tooth. The scumbags must have thought they had the better of me, and I felt a rib crack as one of them got in one last kick.

Cynthia had run out the door shortly after I'd distracted her harasser. One of the small dick boys yelled out that she was getting away, and the six remaining pieces of shit all ran out the door after her.

I crawled toward Josie. Skeeto finally stopped shrieking, and realized he could call 911. Another bar patron leaned over me and asked if I was okay. I spit out a mouthful of blood and groaned "Josie..."

The patron said, "Who?" and I pointed toward my hammer. "Oh!" he said and gently picked up Josie and laid her in my hands. "Do you need an ambulance?"

I just shook my head and crawled to my feet. I had to save Cynthia from those disgusting pieces of shit. I remembered I still had a couple extra Adderall in my purse. I frantically dug for them, then chewed and swallowed, bracing myself against the awful medicine flavor. Almost immediately I felt my strength return. I groaned in pain and heaved myself out the door.

Down the block, the rednecks had Cynthia surrounded. Two of them held her as two more ripped at her dress. I sprinted to them and kicked one of them as hard as I could in the balls. He went down screaming. I swung Josie at a second, smashing his jaw. He croaked and fell to the ground, spitting out teeth, blood, and chunks of bone. The two shitbags holding Cynthia let her go and jumped at me, along with the remaining two redneck scum. Josie ricocheted off one skull and into another's face, just as one of them kicked me on the broken rib. I choked back a scream and twisted in agony. A punch fell on my face and I sucked in my breath and brought Josie down in an arc, into a knee. I shot my elbow up into his face as the redneck bent over in pain. He went down and that left one. I decided this one had to remain conscious and apologize to Cynthia. I twisted his arm around until it popped out of the socket. He howled and I punched him in the gut, sending him to his knees.

I pulled my rope out of my purse and bound the disgusting fuck's hands and feet. Cynthia stood in a doorway, crying. I picked up the redneck by his good shoulder and deposited him in front of her. I kicked him lightly. "Apologize to the lady!"

He spit at her and I knocked him unconscious. I heard sirens and asked Cynthia to help me strip one of them. I tied the clothed rednecks in a circle and laid the naked one in the center. I then leaned each boy over so his mouth was resting on the naked body of their companion. One lucky piece of shit got a surprisingly average-sized dick in his mouth.

I walked Cynthia back to the bar to wait for the police and ran all the way to my camp, here in the woods by the river. I painstakingly stripped out of my dress and climbed down into the river to wash it and myself. After drying off by the fire, I got back into Cinch's clothes and picked up this diary. I think this was a great idea for Cinch, but perhaps I shouldn't write of my adventures as the Pursed Avenger. I still need a better name… I think I'll burn these pages.

Kids Say The Weirdest Things

(By Matt Spencer)

Our neighbors are nice, but a little weird. That's okay. So are we. A few months ago, my husband and I moved into the middle of a three-unit townhouse in a little country village. Spring turned into summer fast, and I'm getting back into shape turning part of the back yard into a little vegetable garden.

The neighbors to our left are quiet and mostly keep to themselves. It's the ones to the right that I wonder about. There's a single mom with a teenage daughter and a cute little boy who's maybe six or seven. The boy has a friend who often comes over and plays, a bouncy little girl his age from down the road. Some nights the lady has some friends over. They play strange music. I've only seen her friends a couple times, showing up and leaving while I'm out on the back porch with insomnia and a cigarette. The lady and her kids don't look or act wealthy, but their friends must be, judging by those fine tailored black suits they always wear. Sometimes they sing along to the music. It's muffled through the walls, not too bothersome, but I do notice. It sounds like some foreign language I can't place. So it's funny that they occasionally complain about the noise my husband makes when he's up late drinking and writing.

The other day, I was out in the garden. It had been a dry couple of weeks, and I sighed in irritation at the wilting edges of the kale and squash I was trying to grow. I thought about using the hose, even though the lady next door would complain about how that drains the well. An SUV pulled into the driveway. I looked up and saw our neighbor get out. She crossed the back yard, to her back porch. Her little boy followed. I remembered them leaving earlier. They'd both been dressed up nice when they left, like they were going to some fancy occasion. I'm pretty sure the boy's little friend from down the road was with them when they left. She wasn't with them now. The mom was still dressed up fancy, but her son now wore plain shorts and a sports T-shirt. He ambled sullenly behind her, like he'd been bad and gotten scolded or spanked. They climbed the steps and went inside. A few minutes later, the mom came back out. She'd changed into shorts, flip-flops, and a tank-top. She started seeing to her flower boxes on her back porch. Before long, the little boy came out and joined her. He looked happier now, laughing and scampering and hopping around, enjoying life like little kids ought to in the summer out in the country, on a day like today. I glanced up with bored interest semi-regularly, from beneath the shadow of my floppy straw sunhat.

Up on the porch, the boy squealed at his mom, "Can I go out and see her?"

I glanced at my struggling crop. The leaves didn't look half so wilted as they had earlier. Maybe it was the light, but they looked like they'd gone a few shades darker green.

I didn't realize the kid was talking about me 'til I heard his Mom say, "No, no, she's busy."

"Please? I wanna go see her! I *like* her!"

My husband was at work, I'd been at my gardening for a while, and I thought overhearing that was so adorable, so I went *What the hell?* "It's okay," I called out, tilting my chin up and putting on my best smile. "He can come say hi!"

His mom said something like, "Okay, you can go say hi, but don't bother her too much."

With a big grin on his face, he bounded down and raced out across the back yard towards me. I kept seeing to my gardening. He trotted to a halt and stood there watching me, like I was the most fascinating thing in the world.

"Hi, how you doing?" I said.

"I'm okay," he said. "I like you."

"I like you too," I said with a giggle.

"Guess what! We went to church today!"

"Is that right?" Oh, yeah, today was Sunday. I hadn't figured them for the church-going sort of family — whatever that is anymore since I was a kid — but okay.

"Yeah. Me, my mom, and Susie."

"Is Susie your little friend I always see you with?" His teenage sister was named Kelly or something. She was out of town this week with some friends, I think I remember hearing. Spring break, or something.

"Yeah," he said.

"What church you guys go to?"

"The one up the dirt road over there." He pointed off to the road that ran down to the left of the house, past a few barns and houses.

"Oh, you mean the one back that way, through the woods?"

"Uh-huh."

"Oh, neat! I've seen that place when I've been out on bike rides. That's a pretty church." It really is a lovely building, the one we were talking about, the old arching colonial sort of structure. "I didn't know we knew anyone who goes there."

"Uh-huh, and today the Priest had me and Susie help him with the ceremony."

Priest? Ceremony? That was a little surprising. I guess I'd just assumed in the back of my mind that the place was something Protestant, so they'd have a pastor or preacher or reverend or whatever. I hadn't seen any Catholic churches around here. Episcopalian, maybe?

I just said, "Wow, cool."

"Yeah. It was a special ceremony, because it's a special day, and the priest said we're special. He put the high scepters at the end of big, long poles, and had us hold them, one of us on each side of him."

"Wow, that's really great! You must be really, really proud and excited."

"Yeah! And you know what else? The priest asked me and Susie which of us wanted to walk in front of him and which one wanted to walk behind him. I wanted to go first, but Susie said she wanted to go first too. So I, I, I let Susie go first. Mom tells me I'm a gentleman. The Priest called me a little gentleman too, so I...I...I wanted to be a gentleman to Susie."

"Well, it sounds like you are, and that's good," I said. "You should keep being a gentleman. Not enough men are."

"Yeah. Do you want to hear about what we did at church?"

I really didn't, but I still said, "Yeah, keep telling me!"

"The Priest, he...he...Once we walked up to the altar, the Priest had me and Susie stand...one on each side of him...up at the...the altar. The Priest read words from the Great Old Book."

"Oh, you mean the Bible?"

"No. The Great Old Book. Anyway, the Priest had me and Susie stand on each side of him while he read the words in the Great Old Book. We were both holding the high scepters up, so the tops of them were above his head while he read. That's a real special thing. Then because Susie walked in front up to the altar, the Priest picked her up and he put her on the altar. The Priest had me help him open Susie up and take things out of her.

"It was...was...It was really scary when Susie screamed. But then she went to sleep, 'and it wasn't scary anymore. It started smelling bad after she stopped screaming. The...the Priest said she was asleep. I was glad she got to sleep. Oh, oh, and then me and the Priest took things out of Susie and put them all around the altar, like the Great Old Book told the Priest how to do. The Priest kept saying words from the Great Old Book while we took stuff out of Susie and we...we...spread her around.

"Then all the lights in the church went kinda dark. So did the lights in the window. The rest of the people out in the benches were saying stuff with us. There were things outside the windows. The things had wings like birds, except they weren't birds, and they had wings like flying dinosaurs have, but they weren't dinosaurs either. They had big wings, and...and...the big things kept flapping their wings on the windows outside. You know what else? It was really messy when we arranged Susie's insides around. Big millipedes came out of the red mess that came out of Susie. The big millipedes took the rest of Susie away. They also took some of the people out in the benches away. The Priest said it was because their faith was weak, but that's good the millipedes took them away too, because now the land of this town is cleaned up of them, and now the town can live on out here for another year.

"You're gonna grow lots of good stuff in your garden now. The dirt's gonna be really, really good all summer, because of what me and Susie and the Priest did when we stood at the altar, and the Priest said the words so the Ones Who Rule The Woods won't be mad at us now for another summer. I'm sad because I won't get to play with Susie for a while anymore."

I didn't know what to say to all that. I guess I just stared at him.

He saw me frowning, and he put his hands in his pockets and shuffled around like he felt guilty, like it dawned on him that he shouldn't have told me about all that. He met my eyes again, pouted for a second, then turned and ran back across the yard, up his porch, and into the house.

Not knowing what to make of all that, I took another look at my garden's yieldings. Now that the little guy mentioned it, the kale looked twice as full as before, and my squashes had swelled and ripened already.

Green Wives Say The Weirdest Things

We moved into the middle of three apartments in this huge house in a small town a few months ago. The couple to our left are alright. They keep to themselves mostly. I have a beer occasionally with the guy. It's the people on the other side that weird us out. It's a single mom and two kids, a teenager and a young boy, maybe six or seven. They go to some church on Sundays, and we hear weird music playing from next door every so often when they have friends over.

The mother complained about me making noise when I'm up late writing, so it's kind of ironic that they do these weird chants at all hours. My wife is usually asleep during them, so she didn't understand at first why I laughed so hard when she told me about the complaint.

Did I mention I'm working on a story about a guy and his dog? They're zombies. I didn't say the wife and I were exactly normal, did I? She dyes her hair purple and pink and has some piercings. I don't need any of that to freak people out, myself.

Anyway, the wife told me about a weird conversation she had with the neighbor's kid today. They went to church and sacrificed a little girl, and giant millipedes crawled out of her and ate some people, or something. I don't know, the kid obviously has quite the imagination.

So yeah, when I got home from work she told me about that, and told me to look at the garden. It's grown up quite a bit since last week. That's great. She's doing a bang-up job. I can't wait to have dinner. Ratatouille tonight, one of my favorite things she does with her garden. Mm-mmmm!

~

After dinner, my wife had a freakout. She went to take a shower and found a weird, greenish rash on her stomach. I told her to go to the doctor first thing tomorrow. I went outside for a cigarette a few minutes ago, and I swear I heard someone whispering in the garden. Those neighbors sure are strange.

~

Okay, last night I had a crazy dream. I think I'm going to have to turn it into a story. I woke up, lying on my back, but I wasn't on the bed, I was about six inches above it. I was held up by all these vines and branches. They held me very tenderly, like I was their baby. I think I felt one stroking my back. They started telling me it was almost time for the winged creatures to be free, and then I could go home.

When I woke up this morning, there was a squash leaf on the pillow where my wife had been. It must have been stuck in her hair when she went to bed. It sure did freak me out for a second.

Wait a second, didn't she take a shower last night?

~

Today at work, a few people said I was acting weird, like I was in some kind of fog. I swear someone was fucking with me. I kept thinking I heard whispers, about wings and a church...This is some fucked up joke someone's playing on me. If it's the wife I suppose I can forgive her, but it's not so funny if it messes with my job, you know?

~

I had to make my own dinner tonight. The wife was working in her garden all evening. When I went out for a cigarette, the neighbor kid was helping her. It sounded like they were singing. I'm glad they get along. My wife doesn't have many friends. I mean, yeah, it's a little kid, but any social interaction is good for her.

~

This morning my wife said she's going to church with the neighbors this week. She has never been religious. In fact, she was a diehard atheist when we got married. It was one of the reasons I fell in love with her. I'm not sure how I feel about this.

That green patch has gotten bigger. I asked if she's gone to the doctor yet. She said the neighbor said it was a favorable sign. Oh gahd, now they're getting her into faith healing. This is not good.

~

Last night's dream was a doozy. I was suspended in the air by the vines again, and this time my wife, the neighbor boy, and a tall, thin, freaky looking priest with long, greying hair were standing at the foot of the bed, chanting. The vines told me my wife was the chosen one. They said I had a choice, to join her or wither and die.

The story I'm getting out of these dreams is phenomenal.

~

Alright, the garden is talking to me. I know, it sounds crazy, but I swear it on my mother's grave. I wandered out into the yard while I was out for a smoke break this morning. I heard the peas say to come closer. The kale told me I was bound for Elysium. A cucumber said I would grow my wings and soar with my wife, and we would conquer all we see, with the help of the Cimmerian gods. The butternut squash said we would establish the Cimmerian kingdom on Earth and bring on the Age of Darkness. I think I heard a green bean tell me to run for my life, but I'm not sure.

Am I losing it? Should I go to the hospital?

~

Today the green is creeping up out of my wife's shirt. It's a beautiful shade, like the leaves of a silver birch, with tiny flecks of viridian. She said it doesn't hurt at all. I touched the green patch, and it felt like it was humming a beautiful song. We stood together for a while, with my hand on her stomach, staring into her eyes. I swore it was only five minutes, but when I looked at the clock three hours had passed.

She said we should make love in the garden. I think it was the best sex we've ever had in our three years of marriage. We started out in the dirt, but the vines lifted us up while she rode me. We climaxed together ten feet in the air. When the vines gently lowered us to the ground, I looked up, and the neighbor kid was standing there, watching. I yelled at him to get the hell out of there. He stared for a few more minutes, then ran off. You'd think the wife and I would have gone in right away, but we just lay there, in the garden.

As the kid got to his porch, we heard him yell, "Mommy they committed the Alzenpadun! We're going to get to see the gods!"

I said, "What the hell is an Alzenpadun?"

My wife just smiled. Oh well, the kid is weird, after all.

~

Tonight we're going to church. It's only Thursday, but my wife said it's time.

~

My wife and I arrived at the church to a full congregation. We paused in the doorway, and everyone turned to look at us. When they looked at my wife, their eyes all began to glow green that matched the patch on her skin. I turned to look at her and gasped. She had turned green from head to toe. Her skin flickered with sparkles of viridian and blinding white, like standing under some tropical canopy, staring up at the sunlight leaking through the leaves.

I felt a small hand grasp mine. I looked down, and it was a little girl with curly brown hair, wearing a green dress that uncannily matched the shade of my wife's new skin. She pulled at my hand and I followed. She led me up the aisle to the left front pew and motioned for me to sit. I complied. She put a finger to her lips to tell me to be quiet, then ran back to her parents a few rows down. I turned to look back at my wife. She was holding a huge scepter, about eight feet tall. Behind her stood the freaky looking priest from my dream. I wasn't surprised. Someone short stood behind the priest, because all I could see was a second scepter rising above his head.

My wife began walking up the aisle. A few paces behind, the priest followed. I saw that the neighbor's boy was the one holding the other scepter. He waited a few paces to start walking behind the priest. They proceeded to the altar, where my wife and the boy stood one to each side of the priest. He picked up a thick, dusty book and began to read in some strange language. After he was done, he gestured to my wife, and she lay down on the altar. I was mesmerized. The priest lifted a golden dagger with a green jewel in the pommel to my wife's chest. I wasn't afraid. As he slowly inserted the knife into her abdomen just below her sternum, my wife screamed. It sounded like beautiful music. The priest cut down her abdomen, then cut around inside her and pulled out her liver. My wife screamed one more time, then passed out. The priest chanted as he removed her organs one by one and placed them around the altar. Finally he reached under her rib cage and cut out her heart.

As he held the heart up, he screamed, "Alesphahendra arise!"

Bright green, viridian, and white light suddenly streamed up from my wife's remains. Her body and organs began to melt and bubble into a puddle on the altar. The puddle began to steam, which created intricate patterns in the light streaming up. Suddenly a hand began to rise from the puddle, then another. As the head emerged, the arms began to spread until they were straight out, like the figure rising from the puddle had been crucified on an invisible cross. The breasts emerged, then the torso. As the figure's hips rose from the altar, she unfurled massive, scaled, blue wings. Once she had risen completely from the puddle, Alesphahendra floated in the air for a moment, until the light streaming up from the altar abated. She slowly floated down to stand in front of the priest. He spread his arms and bowed low. She nodded, then when he had straightened back up, she thrust a hand into his chest. He screamed as she pulled her hand out, clutching his dripping, beating heart. The priest collapsed to the ground. As his body hit the floor, it split open, and six giant black, segmented insects with thousands of legs crawled from the corpse. They devoured the body, then squirmed to Alesphahendra. They climbed her legs, coiling around her body lovingly.

I stood and removed my shirt. Finally, I unfolded my own wings and stretched them to their full length. I held out my hand for Alesphahendra. She took it in her grasp and we walked down the aisle, hand in hand, to the door. Once outside, she raised her arms and thousands upon thousands of the giant millipede-like creatures emerged from the earth, squirming off in every direction. We flew into the sky, still hand in hand, my queen and I. We were joined by beasts with scaled, leathery wings. They swooped and swirled in the sky, and rained fire from their breaths down onto everything below. One of the creatures flew up to me, and held a finger to its mouth, as if to tell me to be quiet, then it flew off.

~

I am free. I float on the wind and watch cities burn. The Scolopendra devour the unrighteous. The Corcodillus Vespertilio soar next to me and my queen. Alesphahendra has risen.

www.ingramcontent.com/pod-product-compliance
Lightning Source LLC
Chambersburg PA
CBHW021846130726
47988CB00009B/3441